NATIONAL FICTION
RESERVE SCHEME

D1740278

THE MACINTYRE PLOT

Walking over the fog-bound moors, ex-policeman Martin Metcalfe found a dead pilot, still strapped in the seat of his plane. He also found a briefcase which was filled with £24,000 in cash! Martin decided to hand it in to the authorities, but as he walked away from the scene of the crash, an armed man was lying in wait to take the cash from him. Metcalfe found himself unwittingly involved in murder, blackmail and high-level intrigue, a situation that called for all his expertise and police knowledge.

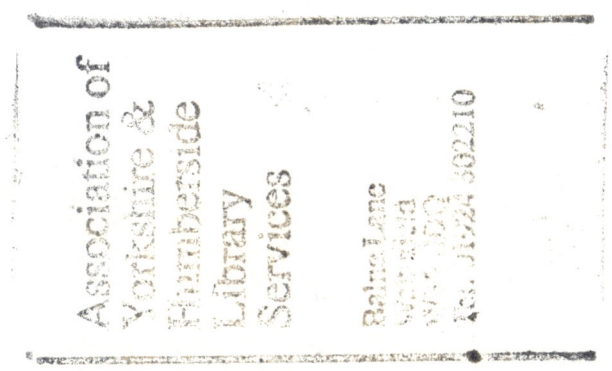

Association of
Yorkshire &
Humberside
Library
Services

THE MACINTYRE PLOT

by

Nicholas Rhea

Dales Large Print Books
Long Preston, North Yorkshire,
England.

British Library Cataloguing in Publication Data.

Rhea, Nicholas
   The MacIntyre plot.

   A catalogue record for this book is
   available from the British Library

   ISBN 1-85389-830-9 pbk

First published in Great Britain by Robert Hale Ltd., 1977

Copyright © 1977 by Peter N. Walker

Cover illustration by arrangement with Last Resort Picture
Library

The moral right of the author has been asserted

Published in Large Print 1998 by arrangement with Peter
Walker

All rights reserved. No part of this publication may be
reproduced, stored in a retrieval system, or transmitted in any
form or by any means, electronic, mechanical, photocopying,
recording or otherwise, without the prior permission of the
Copyright owner.

Dales Large Print is an imprint of
Library Magna Books Ltd.
Printed and bound in Great Britain by
T.J. International Ltd., Cornwall, PL28 8RW.

ONE

I was somewhere in the middle of the cold and desolate North Yorkshire moors surrounded by a thick white blanket of freezing fog. Visibility was totally obscured by this icy curtain of suspended moisture. My clothes and shoes were saturated, and beneath my feet was frozen snow, interspaced with sodden patches of dark brown earth. I was cold, I was soaking and I was utterly alone.

You'll be wondering what I was doing here in the middle of January. I'd come to get out of the house, that's all. I'd set my heart on a short, snappy hike on a beautiful winter's day, and it had been a sunny, albeit chilly, afternoon as I'd parked in Scugdale. I'd climbed the rocky escarpment which led to Scugdale Moor and had located the track which would take me due north. It meandered across the windswept heights, side-stepping bogs, marshes and water courses as it pushed its narrow way through deep maturing heather and acres of bracken, dead already and bronzed against the dark earth.

I'd come because I'd wanted to escape the silent reminders of my dead Julie; I wanted to avoid looking at her photograph which I kept on the mantelpiece. I wanted to avoid being within our marital home without her and the children, so I'd driven out here, only thirty minutes from the village. I simply wanted to walk alone—and I'd never been more alone in my life!

I began to curse my stupidity. I was frightened—I realised I was a bloody fool. If I did get lost, I would grow cold, tired and hungry. I would walk in endless circles and the exposure would eventually chill my body. The bitter mist would aid its work and if I wasn't careful, I'd finish up with hypothermia. And that could prove fatal. I had to keep moving.

The fog had descended so rapidly it had caught me by surprise; I shouldn't have been caught, I know, but I had. It was as simple as that. I'd pressed on, thinking it would clear and now I was slap-bang in the middle of that unnerving mist. It had blotted out all noises and all vision; it covered me like a monstrous parachute.

I'd not been aware of any wind until now, but there it was, hissing through my hair as I walked across that eerie world. I bowed my head against it and droplets cascaded from my uncovered head and ran down my face to disappear among my clothes. I could feel the bite of the easterly wind and my ears were beginning to ache with the persistent cold.

As I walked, I brushed some of the moisture from my clothes and found it was forming tiny icicles on my moustache and among my hair. Three o'clock. With a good Sunday lunch inside me, I was well fortified for the time being. Day-light would remain until around four-thirty this evening, by which time I should be off these hills. I must get down before the temperature dropped any further. On a normal walk, I'd have plenty of time, but in a fog like this you can walk for hours and finish up where you started, going around in circles.

I thought I knew where I was. I was sure I was on the right path, heading for Carlton Bank Top and I reckoned it would be little over a mile from here. I could always catch a bus from there, back to the car. I plodded forward.

As I moved through this silent world I became aware of a shape directly ahead, an indistinct object immediately in front of me. I stopped and rubbed my eyes. The fog can play some funny tricks. But it *was* that grey saloon! It was the vehicle that had taken Julie and the children from me, the speeding monster which had killed them and which had failed to stop. A coward among killers, an untraced villain.

But it couldn't be, not up here! I strained my eyes as I peered at the vague outline. I rubbed them to convince myself that I wasn't dreaming because during the past months I'd thought so much about the grey saloon that I'd seen it in my sleep *and* in my day-dreaming moments. It couldn't be *that* car! Since the accident, I'd inspected every grey saloon that I'd found—and I'd found a lot. I'd spent hours examining them for any evidence of recent repairs or collision damage, and I knew the police had circulated the killer's description too. It wasn't a particularly good description but was the best they had and they'd done all in their power to track him down. Somehow, he'd evaded them and for three months I'd lived with that bloody illusion, my brain hating every living fibre of that lunatic murdering driver, the man who'd destroyed my family and ruined my life.

But this couldn't be a car! It would be a large rock, an outcrop of granite protruding from the dark heather and highlighted by the silvery sheen of accumulated water which clung to the lichens growing upon it. An illusion, a sort of foggy mirage. I remained stationary for a few moments, trying to disassociate my mind from Julie's accident, trying to tell myself that it could not be that grey car. I'd never find *any* saloon up here, let alone the very one I sought. I must control my vivid and over-worked imagination. I couldn't bring them back—no dream was that real and my dream could only be rocks. Lifeless, immobile chunks of grey rock.

I took a deep breath and continued. And as I approached, I saw that it wasn't rock. It was definitely a metallic object. I ran towards it, heart thumping and a new excitement began to course through my veins as I discovered a light aircraft.

Its body lay broken and scattered among the heather and rocks; the fuselage appeared to jut from the earth but was supported from beneath by a large and newly scarred piece of granite. There was a crack down one side of the fabric, like a crack in the shell of an egg and I could smell fuel. There'd surely be no danger from fire because it must have crashed some time ago—I'd heard nothing recently. The fog can muffle sounds to a remarkable degree but I was sure I'd have heard this one miles away. How long had I been walking here? An hour? I could swear there'd been nothing in that time and reckoned it had probably crashed before I'd reached the heights.

My natural curiosity overcame any fear that I might have experienced and I found the pilot. He was quite dead, and still strapped to his seat. I knew he was dead. I've seen countless bodies and no man could survive with a neck bent at that angle. By reaching through the open door, the one on the port side, I could touch his left arm. There was no pulse and his skin was very cold, although rigor mortis had not yet set in. So it was a recent crash—a very recent one. I walked around the wreck, my past training taking over as I found myself making a mental note of everything I saw.

It was a side-by-side two-seater but the starboard seat was empty with no indication that it had been occupied on this flight. The pilot always occupies the port side—and he was still in it with his face bloody and cut and his neck broken.

His door was open and the damage it had sustained suggested it had been thrown open upon impact. The plane's nose, which housed its solitary propellor driven engine, had come into violent contact with the earth. It had been crushed upon impact and its heavy contents had been thrust back into the cockpit to trap and break the pilot's legs. The plane's wheels lay nearby, a nose-wheel and two landing wheels, all of which had been wrenched off in its moment of landing upon this roughest of terrain. The aircraft was silver coloured with red underparts and the paint looked and indeed smelled very new. Strangely it bore no registration number. I looked around the fuselage and beneath the wings for the large letter 'G' which should have been painted there and which would have told me it was a U.K. registered aircraft. Had it been there, it would have been followed by a hyphen and four capital Roman letters. But there were no markings—every aircraft should bear them to indicate its country of registration. I next sought the fireproof metal plate; this should be fixed on the fuselage near the main door to provide the name and address of the owner. But there was no plate on this one, although I did find the rivet holes where it should have been. I guessed the plane was in the middle of being re-painted—the plate had possibly been removed for that reason, and that would explain the absence of its registration letters. They'd be temporarily hidden beneath its new coat, awaiting the art of a sign-writer.

To fly without them was illegal and it would be difficult to trace ownership; I hoped the pilot carried some form of identification. Actually, it may be possible by checking the direction indicator and the maps to discover the origin of its flight. But none of that was my responsibility any more—I needn't start worrying about that sort of thing!

I recognised the model as the Bulldog 100, a useful private plane with a range of around 600 miles and an average cruising speed of some 120 mph. But this one would fly no more.

I knew better than to touch anything inside. The pilot was beyond human aid but I peered into the wrecked interior to see if there were any valuables which ought to be taken into safe custody. Other than maps, I found nothing, not even the pilot's log, although he wouldn't need one if he was on an internal flight within U.K. boundaries.

My remaining duty as a citizen was to summon help, and, after taking a final look at the silent wreckage, I began to walk away. It was only then that I spotted the brief-case. It lay close to the port wing and nestled among the thick heather. It was one of those black, solid-looking types with chrome lips, solid and rectangular in shape; it was about 3″ deep, looked good and gave the 'executive' touch to lesser mortals like salesmen and office workers. I decided I could touch this. The rules governing plane crashes demanded that no wreckage be touched until the Board of Trade or the Civil Aviation Authority had attended to examine it, but luggage or personal property which was scattered about could be removed for safe custody.

Gingerly, I lifted the case. It was moderately heavy and bore the initials 'P.B.G.' in white paint upon the lid. I laid it on the ground, crouched before it and pressed the twin catches. I half expected it to be locked, but the lid flew open.

It was packed with money.

TWO

I must have stared at its contents for an entire minute. They were crisp new notes, all wrapped in their paper bands and just there for the taking. I removed one of the wads, handling it as if it was a piece of fragile china and scarcely believing my luck. It comprised five pound notes, one hundred in number if the label was telling the truth and I had no reason to doubt it. The wads were stacked four deep; that made £2,000 in each pile and the wads were six deep along the front with an equal amount to the rear of the case. That made £24,000! In cash!

I'd never seen so much money; I could smell it. The distinctive scent of paper money was stronger even than the earthy pungency of the saturated ground and dying bracken in which it lay. And there was so much! I delved among the wads with both hands and pressed the tightly packed notes to my face to savour that gorgeous scent. A lot of them dropped to the ground as my nervous hands tried to seize too much, and then, when the case was almost empty, I found more. This was in loose fivers spread across the bottom and it totalled a further thousand pounds. It had apparently been placed there because there hadn't been room for it as wads.

As I returned each wad to the case, I closely examined them, suspecting that their innards may be pieces of newspaper or something similar. But it was all real money, every solitary piece. And I know money when I see it!

So here was I, out of work and sitting in a clump of heather with £25,000 in my lap. It was the heaven-sent solution to all my problems—I could pay off the mortgage and invest the residue, which would provide a moderate income, maybe enough to live on if I was well advised by my bank. I could spend my days seeking that grey saloon and its driver; I could make it my life's quest without the eternal worry of having to find money by earning a living.

I realised I was alone with this knowledge —if there had been a passenger (and I was sure there hadn't) he'd have retrieved this case before seeking help. The case wasn't hidden—any fool would have seen it even in this fog, but I made a second recce just to make sure no one else was lying nearby, dead or injured. There wasn't.

I snapped shut the lid. I put every note back in the case—some were wet and soiled but that didn't matter—and I rose to my feet. The case, not unduly heavy, hung at my side and my right hand clutched the handle as if never to release it. But even before I left the scene, my honest rural upbringing and my past training began to gain authority over my initial dishonest intention. I found myself thinking of the dead pilot and his family. Perhaps he had children? They'd lost their dad—I knew how they'd feel, having just lost my children. This might be their money. Maybe their entire future depended upon this cash—it might be all they had to pay for food and clothing now and in the future. I knew perfectly well that I had no right to it. It would be outright theft on my part if I retained it and sooner or later someone would seek it. You couldn't hope to conceal the disappearance of such a large amount.

If it vanished from here, there'd be a massive enquiry which would embrace the whole of this remote countryside and someone was likely to remember seeing my car, now parked in Scugdale, or seeing me walk upon the path to these heights. I knew only too well how the county police could comb an entire area of this nature, and I also knew how the local people paid close attention to strangers. Already, my car would have received a careful scrutiny by the Scugdalers and it would be a topic of conversation over their teas tonight. They'd wonder who it was and why I was in the area, and when news of the crash filtered to them they'd associate me and my car with it.

Apart from the beginning of my hike, I must descend from the moor and in that I would surely be seen. Someone would spot me and note my appearance—villagers and farmers hereabouts take a natural interest in persons walking alone. I'd be remembered all right, especially as I was dressed in my Sunday best! On the return

I'd be carrying a brief-case too—a real picture in the middle of these moors!

Call me a coward if you like, or say that I lacked fibre, but I decided to do the honourable thing. My conscience wouldn't allow me to do otherwise, so I turned away from the wreckage and took the brief-case with me for safe keeping. I would hand it over to the police when I reported the crash; many men in my situation would have kept it, I know. Some would have risked discovery and interrogation, but not me. Pinching £25,000 is a far cry from borrowing a paper clip from the office or taking a brick from a building site. Besides, the whole affair reeked of mystery—I thought of blackmail, tax evasion or an undercover business deal and knew that many activities, illicit or otherwise, depended upon the availability of hard cash. If this was a dishonest operation which had misfired, the owners of this money would leave no stone unturned to get it back and their methods could be equally dishonest or even downright dangerous. I knew I'd made the right decision; I'd have peace of mind even if I remained broke!

I walked for almost another hour during

which the fog never lifted one inch nor receded one yard. By now, I was thoroughly drenched and my shoes squelched gallons of bitterly cold water through the lace holes but absorbed an equal amount through their fabric. The intense chill of these hills had started to attack my body through my saturated clothes and those minutes of inactivity about the plane hadn't helped. I was bloody frozen! My feet were like blocks of ice—when your toes are cold, you feel cold all over. I increased my pace, hoping to maintain a reasonable level of heat within my body. The cold made my ears ache at their tips, for the temperature must be well below freezing now. My face was frozen into immobility and the hand which clutched the case was stiff and cold. I kept the other in my coat pocket where at least it was shielded from the bitter wind, and the case constantly changed hands.

The path began to descend and the fog cleared a fraction. Then, quite suddenly, I was walking across a flat, unmade surface of earth; it appeared to be longer and wider than a football pitch and I knew where I was. I'd reached the gliding club's unpaved runway. It lay close to the summit of Carlton Bank and belonged to a comparatively new gliding club whose members hadn't seen the need to build a surfaced landing strip. This makeshift airfield was popularly used by gliders and I knew that small planes could also land here, as indeed many did.

It was more than a mere possibility that the Bulldog had been making for this lofty place; he'd crashed on the moors, a common occurrence when flying below 3,000 feet because your altimeter can give false readings due to the changes in barometric pressures. These vary from place to place; when flying within the British Isles it's easy for even the most experienced pilot to make an error when travelling the length of the country, simply due to the changing pressures brought about by the natural features of the landscape. An error as small as one millibar can be fatal by causing an aircraft to crumple into a mountainside or a hilltop. He thinks he's flying higher than he is—and an error of only thirty feet is the difference between life and death.

The fog makes a pilot little better than a blind man and he must rely upon his instruments. And they'd failed him, poor devil.

Anyway, here was I with a fortune in my frozen hands, squelching across the foggy, muddy and deserted acres of this small airfield. I couldn't see the distant extremities so I walked in what I hoped was a straight line and eventually came to the heathery verge at the far side. I decided to follow the verge as it led off to my left and, happily, I'd chosen correctly because I came upon the junction with the steep slip-road. Like the landing strip into which it led, it was unsurfaced and descended from this plateau to a minor surfaced road which I knew well. I located the white painted marker stones which indicated the outer edges of the slip-road and began my final descent with muddy, yellow water running at my feet. I was bitterly cold but felt safe, although it was a further five hundred yards to the public road.

Some five minutes later I emerged through the gate which marked the gliding club's boundaries and found myself on the friendly tarmac surface. I could have kissed it! This narrow moorland road runs from the village of Chop Gate in Bilsdale, across the heights, down Carlton Bank, into Carlton Village and eventually joins the A.19 trunk road. In summer, the minor road is busy because this hilltop is a popular beauty spot and on a clear day it commands outstanding views over North Yorkshire, Cleveland, Durham and even to the Pennines. But today, the vantage point offered no more than any other part of my journey across the summit and a stranger wouldn't have realised he was standing on such a lofty aspect. But even today, the beauty spot wasn't entirely deserted. In spite of the cold and fog, a car was standing at the roadside, a solitary visitor on this singularly unromantic and awesome afternoon. At first, the vehicle was no more than a mere outline in the mist, but as I approached, I saw it was a Ford Escort, pale blue and in average condition. There was a man in the driving seat; his back was against the window and the engine was running. He'd be keeping himself warm as he read the newspaper. This was just the chap to run me to the nearest police station!

I had to admire his determination to gain solitude, for he couldn't have chosen a more remote and private place if he'd tried. He seemed utterly disinterested in the scenery and I wondered why he'd elected to come here. I was close to him, level with his car, and was about to tap on his window when he turned and saw me. He cast his *News of the World* to the floor and leapt out, obviously in a hurry and very anxious to confront me.

Even more surprising was the brief-case he carried. The initials it bore were the same as mine; it was an exact duplicate in colour, size and style.

'I've been waiting for bloody hours!' he snapped, climbing out of the warm car. 'It's enough to freeze a brass monkey up here! Is that the money? The gen's in here. I didn't hear you land. The fog's bloody thick, isn't it? I was beginning to think you weren't going to make it—I was going to give you another half hour, that's all, and then I'd have had to leave, money or no money.'

He placed his brief-case at my feet and before I could gather my wits, he reached for mine. I pulled away.

'Just a minute!' I cried. 'Who the hell are you?'

'Come off it!' he growled, eyeing me carefully. 'We don't give names. We just obey instructions.'

I stood my ground. 'I'm not handing this

23

over unless you can prove you're entitled to it.'

'Look,' he said. 'This is no time to act bloody stupid. I've been sent to pick up that case and to deliver this one. And that's what I'm going to do.' And to emphasise his point, he pulled a stubby Walther automatic from his pocket, its muzzle pointing directly at my chest. 'Come on,' he urged. 'Hand it over. You're wasting precious time.'

Once more he reached for my case and my poor frozen fingers couldn't tighten their grip. I wanted to back off, but the gun said no. Watching me like a hawk, he removed it from my hand.

'There,' he said with a quick smile. 'I was hoping this wasn't a double-cross.' He squatted on his haunches in the middle of the road, flicked open the lid and riffled the cash. 'Thanks. The gen's in my case—it's accurate. We've checked.' He closed his lid.

Having satisfied himself, he returned to his car, slammed the door and drove off with the £25,000.

'Hey!' I ran after him, trying desperately to read his number as the Escort was swallowed in the swirling mist. It had

24

been an expert and well-planned switch. The fellow must have some claim to the cash because he knew of its arrival, yet hadn't realised I was not the true carrier. The whole thing was so bloody odd and so unreal that it seemed like a dream. But this was no dream.

It was so real that I now had his car number, and with difficulty managed to write it on an old envelope from my wallet. It was PXC 185J, and I added the date, time and place, plus a brief description of the car and its driver.

He was male, aged about thirty, with long dark brown hair, clean shaven and had good teeth. Those teeth remained clear in my mind's eye, for they were extraordinarily strong and white. He wore a suede car coat over dark grey trousers. All this went into my note in a spidery sort of writing due to the immobility of my chilled fingers. But I could read it, and that's what mattered.

The duplicate brief case stood in the road where he'd left it, so I picked it up, half-expecting it to be as heavy as the one I'd released. It turned out to be very light with an empty feeling; I carried it to the side of the road and placed it on a heap of gravel where I pressed the catches. Like the other, the lid opened at a touch but inside this one I found only a buff coloured envelope, foolscap size. It was unmarked but sealed.

I fingered it carefully, most wary in case it contained an explosive device. It was barely bulky enough and the contents appeared to be nothing more than a single sheet of thin paper. Although my hands lacked their usual sensitivity, I was sure there were no wires, springs, pieces of cardboard or plastic inside. I decided to open it.

Inside, I found a piece of ordinary white paper, quarto size and folded twice which I spread in the trough of the case. It bore a single word 'ENGLAND' written in capitals, and following that was what appeared to be a computer reference. The figures were 7511651700-45444994. The sheet was blank on the reverse side. There was nothing else; I checked the case for hidden compartments and ran my fingers around the inside to feel for catches or other objects, but I drew a blank.

I laboriously copied those details onto

my piece of scrap and returned the sheet and its envelope to the case. I could now report the entire incident to the authorities, hand in the case and contents and have something to think about during my idle moments!

I started the long walk down Carlton's steep and twisting bank and by the time I'd descended a couple of hundred feet, the visibility had improved. I was leaving the foggy cloud behind and began to stride briskly along the hard surface, walking as quickly as I could until my body began to grow a few degrees warmer. Down here, the icy wind had lost much of its bite and I was even beginning to enjoy the exercise. It wasn't long before a motorist stopped to offer a lift—I said I'd appreciate a lift to Stokesley because I wanted to find the police station.

It is a quaint and rather grimy building, situated in the middle of this old market town and it has a blue 'Police' sign outside. I entered to find myself at a small counter which blocked the tiny entrance hall and upon it was a bell push which I pressed. A mature constable, with whom I was not acquainted, attended to me and I told him the entire story, albeit in a condensed form. Because of my involvement, he said I'd have to make a statement, in writing and thought that someone of senior rank may wish to interview me. He'd have to ring up about that.

I told him that I could write out the statement without his aid and would do it while he did his telephoning. I told him I'd been a policeman in York until only three months ago, when I resigned.

'What did you say your name was?'

'Metcalfe,' I said. 'Martin James Metcalfe. I resigned when my wife and family got killed in a road accident. I couldn't see the point in working, so I chucked it in. I think I jumped the gun, but I'm stupid like that, always acting on impulse and then regretting it! Anyway, my domestic worries are no concern of yours—get me a statement form and I'll write out the full story for your files.'

'Was that hit-and-run yours? The grey car we've all been looking for?'

'That's the bastard. And I'll track him down if it's the last thing I do, so help me!'

'We turned over every one in Stokesley and district. We knew it was a copper's

28

family—we did our best for you.'

'Thanks.'

He disappeared and returned with the necessary Form 38 and several continuation sheets in case I wrote a lot. He showed me into an office which doubled as the interview room and although it was sparsely furnished, there were the basic essentials. I sat at the desk and began to write in long-hand as he disappeared, with the brief-case, to contact those who would have to cope with the crashed aircraft, the sudden death it had presented, and the problem of tracing the gunman who'd relieved me of the cash.

It took half-an-hour to compile the statement and I included everything in chronological order. I carefully read it through, made one or two minor alterations, signed it and carried it through to him. He was on the phone, clearly talking to a 'sir', so I waited.

'That was our inspector,' he said as he concluded. 'He says our C.I.D. will deal with the matter of the money and the death; he'll make sure they are told. We'll sort out the crash side of the incident and we needn't detain you any longer. If we want you again, we'll contact you.'

I handed the statement to him and he glanced through it, saying 'Thanks. It's all in here.'

'My car's in Scugdale. Is there a bus route anywhere near there?'

'Buses run regularly from here to Swainby. You could get off at Swainby and walk —it's only a short distance from there to Scugdale. The buses wait in the square to the right of this station—you'll see the time-table. I'd run you over to Scugdale myself, but I can't leave the office until we get this lot sorted out. You know how these things cause a flap.'

'I do. And don't worry, I'll get a bus. Do your cafés open on Sundays?'

'There's one overlooking the bus terminus. Turn right outside our door—you'll see the lights.'

I thanked him and left. I enjoyed the hot cooked meal in spite of my damp clothes and now felt much warmer and happier. My adventure was over and I'd done my duty. It was back to normality for me, so I caught a bus and hiked from Swainby to my waiting car. It was just after nine o'clock when I got home. I jumped straight into a hot bath, got changed into something dry and casual, and went over

30

to the White Swan for my night-cap—two pints of best bitter.

I needed something to make me sleep now that I had no Julie to cuddle and two pints is a very, very poor substitute.

I might even make it three tonight.

THREE

Somebody was trying to rouse me. I tried to ignore the noise by pulling the sheets over my head and hoped he'd go away. But he didn't. He persisted with a rhythmic beating; whoever it was certainly knew how to knock people out of bed for it seemed as if the entire house was vibrating through his efforts. My visitor was pounding on the front door, using a clenched fist by the sound of it and such was his determination that I began to fear for the safety of my woodwork. I lived in an old cottage which needed constant attention to varying parts of it, especially its rotting door frames!

'All right, all right, I'm coming,' I shouted. 'Don't knock the place down!'

It was one hell of an effort to sit up

because I'd had four pints, not three, and the sleep seemed to weigh heavily upon me. It tried to press me back into the cosy warmth but the terrible hammering persisted and won the day. I threw off the bedclothes, pushed myself into a sitting position and pulled at the cord to switch on the light. I managed to locate my slippers and staggered around the foot of the bed towards the door where I collected my dressing gown from its hook.

Wrapping it about my bare torso, I trudged downstairs and lit my way at which the knocking stopped. I allowed myself a few seconds in the kitchen where I stood in the middle of the floor and took deep breaths to clear my swimming head. I didn't even glance at the time as I crossed the lounge and switched on the light. Then I made sure I switched on the exterior light to reveal my visitor. I also illuminated my tiny entrance hall.

Outside stood two men I'd never seen before. They were tall and one was noticeably slim. He acted as spokesman.

'Mr Metcalfe?' his opening words were polite enough.

'Yes?' I ran a hand through my hair and yawned apologetically.

'Can we come in?' he requested.

'Who are you? What do you want?' I was cautious, naturally, as I shivered in the icy blast.

He produced a warrant card and said, 'Police—we're from the Special Branch.'

I tried to examine his card but he slipped it back into his wallet as he awaited my reaction.

'You'd better come in,' I wanted to shut out the chilliness, for already millions of goosepimples were crowding upon my chest. They stepped inside.

In the warmth of my lounge, I noticed it was just after two o'clock in the morning. What a bloody time to call! But the police did that—they called when it suited them, not when it suited the customer.

'Before we start,' I decided to check their identities again, 'can I see your warrant cards? I didn't get a proper look out there.'

The thin one looked at his colleague and smiled grimly, showing uneven teeth. 'We've got a suspicious one here, Joe,' but he produced his. It was a Metropolitan Police warrant card in the name of Detective Sergeant Peter Riley; his colleague, a heavily built man about thirty years old, produced a similar card in the name of Detective Constable Joseph Pierce.

'Thanks, sit down.' I looked at each man in turn as I awaited some enlightenment.

Riley spoke.

'You discovered and reported a crashed plane on the moors, Mr Metcalfe. We have been in touch with Stokesley Police and they gave us your name and address. We'd like to hear your account please.'

'I gave all the details at Stokesley.'

'Yes, I know, but we'd like to hear the story from you, in person; it is important, I assure you, otherwise we wouldn't have knocked you out of bed.'

'Can I fix coffee for us all before you start?' My mouth felt like a drain and they said they'd love one. I brewed a pot full and settled it before us as I gave my account. It was virtually a repetition of my earlier statement and they asked very few questions at that stage.

'Were you expecting the arrival of that aircraft, Mr Metcalfe?' Riley asked when I'd finished, and there was a distinct chill in his voice.

'Expecting it? What the hell do you mean? I knew nothing about it until I stumbled across it.'

'It seems odd that you decided to take a walk in those uncertain weather conditions when an aircraft just happened to be lying wrecked with £25,000 begging to be collected by a passing hiker.'

'Don't be bloody silly! I've told you how I came to be there. I'd never seen the aircraft before. For God's sake you don't think I'm involved, do you?'

'We don't think anything, Mr Metcalfe. We are simply gathering facts. Now, you walked off with the brief-case. Did you intend keeping it? It must have been very tempting, mustn't it?'

'It was, I don't mind admitting that. But I'm an honest person and had formed the intention to take it to the police long before the fellow with the gun staked his claim.'

'I'd like you to go over that part again—when the fellow in the Escort pointed his gun at you.'

I repeated that part of the incident and included the car's registration number which I'd retained in my memory.

'I put it to you, Mr Metcalfe,' said Riley in those cold tones, 'that you intended to locate and to keep that cash; I put it to you that, somehow, you knew of the Bulldog's impending arrival and that you were aware of its contents. You waited at Carlton to relieve the pilot of the money, but he crashed before landing so you searched those moors until you found the wreckage. Then you took the money. Only the timely intervention of the man for whom it was intended prevented you getting away. And you concealed your true role by pretending to be an innocent hiker and reinforced that by reporting it all to the police.'

I stared at him; there he sat, in my house drinking my coffee and insinuating that I was a villain and that I had lied about my hike. I'm basically a calm person but must admit that I strongly considered throwing him out there and then. Had I not been an ex-policeman, I would have burst into a torrent of loud and angry abuse laced with total denials, and then shown him the door. But I realised that his veiled accusations were all part of his questioning technique. This is frequently done in police circles—you try to get the interviewee upset and angry and you heap unreasonable pressure upon him to make him talk and to say things he never intended. And this character was using those tactics on me. I knew enough not to allow myself to be goaded into anger and certainly I was not going to provide a loophole for them to further suspect me. I made no reply to his outburst; instead, I sipped from my coffee cup and peered at them in turn.

'You've really upset someone's plans, haven't you?' Riley spoke with a hint of sarcasm.

'Plans?' I asked.

'The note you received in exchange. Where is it?'

'I left it at Stokesley Police Station, you know that.'

'What did it say?'

'I've told you. It was a code number on a piece of paper, and there was the word "England". I can't remember the number—it looked like a computer reference and was meaningless to me.'

'Did you try to decipher it?'

'No, I had no reason to try.' I had tried, of course, and had taken that copy of it, but I decided not to tell him about it. To admit I'd done so could indicate that my interest was more than casual and might further implicate me.

'The pilot, one assumes, was to have done exactly as you did,' Riley continued.

'Let us suppose that he was to deliver the money in exchange for that note. Then, having done so, he would return from whence he came and deliver the note to some waiting colleague.'

I said nothing as Riley stared at me.

'Well?' he said.

'Well, what?' I deliberately adopted a blank expression.

'You've interrupted that chain of events, haven't you.'

'No, the crash interrupted it. Had it not been for the crash, things might have proceeded as you suggest.'

'But you were there, conveniently on hand, to intercept the coded number, a number worth £25,000 of someone's cash. By taking a copy of it and then handing it to the police, you have completely ruined someone's plans.'

'I took no copy and I'm not interested in bloody code numbers. I was only doing what any normal honest citizen would have done.' My coffee was growing cold so I topped it up. Pierce, who hadn't spoken, held out his cup and I re-filled it. Riley didn't seem to want any more; he was on the edge of his chair, the eagerness clear on his thin face.

'You could be in danger, you realise that.' He sank back into his seat, his pale eyes blinking at me.

'You clearly know more than I do,' I returned. 'But I can't see why I should be at risk. I'm not involved in any way and if there was a plot, the plotters will know that I'm innocent. So I've nothing to fear.'

'Mr Metcalfe. It would seem to me that someone has gone to a great deal of trouble and expense to prepare that exercise and for them, it has gone terribly wrong. Not only have their plans gone awry, but the object of their operation—the code number —is now in the hands of the police. Those gentlemen, I feel, are the very people into whose possession they would not wish that number to fall. And you are responsible for doing that. By a sheer coincidence you happened to be there, just at the right time, to completely ruin their plans. Do you think they will accept that it happened by coincidence? They'll believe they had an informer in their midst, someone who has been instrumental in ruining the operation. They are bound to feel that you know more than you will ever admit; they'll believe you know their code and how to interpret that number. They'll think you are an agent sent to do exactly that.'

'What was the purpose of the operation?' I ventured. 'Do *you* know something, or is all this mere supposition?'

'We don't know anything, that's why we are here. We want to find out and we think you can help. We'd like to know who was behind it, Mr Metcalfe, and why you had to stop it from succeeding. There are too many coincidences and I don't like coincidences.'

'Oh, for God's sake!' I leapt from my chair and stamped around the room. 'I've told my story and that's all I know. I am not involved in any way. Can't you believe that?'

I'd completed a tour of my furnishings and halted before them. 'I think it's time I asked you a few questions. You are from the Metropolitan Police, so what are you doing up here, in Yorkshire? This is way out of your territory. For an enquiry of this sort, I'd have expected the local force to interview me, not you.'

'We were already in the district, Mr Metcalfe, on a mission which I am not at liberty to divulge. We are interested in this aircraft and its load because it may be connected with our other enquiries.'

'I'm sorry I cannot be more helpful, but surely the local police will give you all the help you need.'

'Not them; you. Well, Joe. I think we can leave Mr Metcalfe for the time being. He can reflect upon his role, for we'll return.'

'Where did the aircraft come from?' I asked as they rose to their feet. They were leaving, thank God; they'd soon opted to depart when I'd turned the tables!

'We don't know. We haven't troubled the local police about that aspect of it. At the moment we are concerned with its reason for being here. Come on, Joe. We've lots more work to do.'

They left as suddenly as they'd arrived. I listened as their footsteps receded down my path and heard the slamming of their car door. As they drove from the village, I rushed into my dining-room to peep from the darkened window, but failed to distinguish their car's colour, make or registration number. It was too far away and accelerating fast.

I locked the door and returned to bed, but before sinking once again into my blissful slumber, I took the coded number from my wallet and, leaning against the headboard, stared at it. 7511651700-45444994 and the word 'England'.

The hyphen may be a hyphen, or it could be a subtraction sign. I attempted a mental subtraction but found I couldn't retain the figures in my mind and my nearest ballpoint pen was on the dressing table. I couldn't be bothered to get out of bed to reach it. For my money, this was a computer reference rather like the one they printed on my phone bill or on the electricity account. I'd have another try tomorrow; my head was too hazy to struggle any more so I slipped it back into my wallet, pushed it under the bed and prepared to drift once more into the arms of Morpheus. But I lay awake for a long time. I heard the parish clock strike four but must have dropped off shortly afterwards.

The morning's *Yorkshire Post* carried a short news item about the crash. I read the account as I ate my toast and marmalade but it didn't say a great deal and restricted itself to a simple factual story which said that a Bulldog aircraft had crashed in fog on Carlton Moor, killing the pilot. There was a photograph of a similar Bulldog in flight but no mention was made of the money nor was the pilot's name revealed. The report said his identity could not be published until the next of kin had been notified and my name did not appear in the account. For that I was thankful.

But I couldn't sit here and read all morning because I had work to do.

The week's dirty linen awaited my attention!

FOUR

That moorland adventure occupied a corner of my mind all that day and Tuesday too, although I neither heard nor read any more about it. On several occasions, I'd tried to work out a meaning of the lengthy figure which, I felt, must be a code. Always, it defeated me. Then, on Wednesday, the village policeman called to warn me that I'd be required as a witness at both the inquest upon the pilot and at the inevitable enquiry by the Civil Aviation Authority, but neither dates had been fixed. This was a preliminary notice, that's all, so that I would be prepared and in a state of constant readiness.

As I brewed coffee, the constable told me that a preliminary investigation had suggested a probable cause of the crash. There had been no mechanical failure so it seemed the aircraft had been flying too low through the pilot's miscalculation of his altimeter. The post mortem on his body had shown the cause of death to be a combination of multiple injuries and shock sustained during the crash; the deceased had been physically fit and had suffered no heart disease or other fatal illness. He didn't know whether a positive identification had yet been made.

I asked if anything had developed about the code and P.C. Curran said he knew nothing about it—he did know that the C.I.D. had been making a lot of enquiries and seemed greatly concerned about the Bulldog; they had established its starting point which was a small airfield in Buckinghamshire. This had been evident from the maps it carried and they showed he'd been heading for Carlton, as I'd thought. The police had failed to trace the blue Ford Escort and it seemed its registration number had never been issued.

Thus another mystery was created. Who was its driver?

Norman Curran knew little else—he was our local bobby and we lived some twenty-five miles from the scene of that crash. The hub of the enquiry was out of his jurisdiction, although he knew a little about it. After exhausting conversation about the mystery, we chatted about my rather bleak and lonely future and he asked if I'd made any progress in the hunt for the murderous grey saloon. We were good friends—I lived in the village where he was bobby and in the time I'd been a serving member in the force, I'd tried not to interfere with his running of the place. My work lay in York, some twenty miles away; I lived here to obtain the benefits of life in rural England and commuted to work like ordinary folks. Law enforcement in the village had been no concern of mine.

After he'd left, I heard nothing further about the crash and it was on Thursday morning that it next entered my mind. It occurred in an odd sort of way, my interest being re-ignited by one of those little things which sets the brain working and which causes past incidents to merge into something tangible. It happened like this. I'd climbed from my bed soon after eight, made breakfast and was reading the book reviews in the *Yorkshire Post* when the mail arrived.

Among the letters was my new driving licence. I'd applied for its renewal about a week ago but now that the Department of the Environment had established the Driver and Vehicle Licensing Centre at Swansea, I found that my local taxation officer had simply issued me with a receipt for the fee and had forwarded my application to the DVLC, who would send my licence. After a suitable lapse of time, during which official wheels ponderously turned, the licence had reached me.

I opened the envelope to examine it. It was green in colour and folded in a transparent plastic cover. At the top was my Driver Number, a coded figure arrived at by juggling with the constituent figures and letters of my date of birth and my name. The licence bore a note which asked me to check my date of birth to ensure that it was correctly printed; it was located in the bottom right hand corner. In my case it was 17th June 1941. This was written as 17.06.41 and was correct.

A printed paragraph said that, having established the accuracy of my date of birth, I was allowed to cut off the corner which bore it and so conceal my age from prying eyes. This is a consideration prized by our lady drivers but being an ex-policeman, I knew that my Driver Number contained my date of birth in code form. My Driver Number was METCA 406171 MJ6Yo.

METCA comprises the first five letters of my surname; for persons with short surnames, like Lee, the necessary spaces are filled with figure 9. Lee would be LEE99. The numerical part of the code is made up from my date of birth. The figures of my *year* of birth (41) are the first and last digits of that code; the *month* of birth (06) accounts for the 2nd and 3rd Digits, and my *day* of birth (17) for the next two, thus making 406171. For lady drivers, though, the figure 5 is always added to the second digit of the complete code. Had I been a woman with my date of birth, my number would be 456171. A woman born on 17.11.1941 would be coded 461171—the added 5 makes the second digit become 6 in this case. This device is a simple method of distinguishing, in paper, the sex of persons whose names may be either feminine or masculine, for example Noel Hilary Sevearne. If her birthday was 1st April 1952, her code would be SEVEA 554012, followed by a further computer reference of internal interest only. If Noel was a man, however, his code would be 504012 ...

That bloody code! The one I'd copied after the crash. Did it contain such a coded date? I dug into my wallet and spread the piece of paper upon the breakfast table. 7511651700-45444994. I counted the first six figures and drew a faint line after them. That gave me 751165. Could this be a date? If a similar system had been utilised, the figure 5 suggested a female. It took a matter of seconds to arrive at 16.01.75. The 16th January 1975. Today!

I checked with my newspaper and sure enough, it was Thursday, 16th January 1975. My heart was thumping by this time—whether it was a coincidence that the figures could be converted to a date remained to be seen, so I tackled the next batch of figures by drawing another stroke after six of them. I chose to divide the total into three batches of six simply because there were eighteen all told, and because the first did made some sort of sense. If this method failed to produce anything viable, I could try others, such as making a division at the hyphen. Anyway, I now had 1700-45.

The date 1700 was highly improbable and my trained mind began to function. 1700. Seventeen hundred. Could it be a time, an indication of the hour?

1700 hours is a universal method of writing 5 p.m. I was undecided how to interpret the dash which followed it. If this was a time, the 1700 minus 45 could suggest quarter past four, but that was a clumsy way of writing it, even in coded form. If they'd wanted to write 4.15 p.m. in this manner, surely they'd have used the figures 1615? A hyphen could mean until—we used it in the police, so could I read this as '5 p.m. until 5.45 p.m.'? I'd try it for starters.

I wrote my diagnosis in the margin of my *Yorkshire Post*—'Thursday, 16th January 1975, between 5 p.m. and 5.45 p.m.'. This made real, exciting sense. I was left with a further six numerals, 444994, and my mind clicked into police procedure. I had a date and a time, so obviously I needed a place. I'd been taught always to

49

note date, time and place of any incident. This had been drummed into me at the training school. Date, time and place. Those three words were impressed upon my mind just as the alphabet is learned by children and remembered by them as adults. If the latter figure represented a location, it must surely be a map reference. It took a policeman's mind to work out this code—had a policeman's mind created it? It was an interesting thought.

I hurried into the lounge and took my collection of Ordnance Survey maps from the shelf. I selected Map No.91 because it contained those references; it was our local map and I found square number 44 and estimated 4/10ths of it. I found 99 too, and estimated 4/10ths of that one too, then joined the two imaginary lines. They met at a road junction on the A.19 road, at a place bang on the site of the Cleveland Tontine Hotel! The hotel is shown on the map and lies some six miles by road from Carlton Bank Top.

I found myself quivering with excitement and wondered just how much of a coincidence this really was. Policemen didn't really accept them, so was I willing the numbers to fit my own unlikely whims and fancies? A mathematician could probably work that long sequence of numerals into something feasible from his own particular angle, whilst an astronomer might read something into it that forecast the path of a comet or calculated the position of a star! But I was—or had been—a policeman, trained up to the eyeballs at Newby Wiske to record the date, time and place of any incident, and to think logically. And I'd found a date, a time and a place! What's more, it seemed so relevant to the crashed aircraft. I knew that my conclusions, erratic though they might be, would have to be checked. But by whom?

The word 'England' seemed pretty obvious; I felt that someone was to meet a colleague in England at the Cleveland Tontine, between 5 p.m. and 5.45 p.m. today. You may well read something else into that coded numeral. On reflection, the person *would* have been going to meet his colleague there.

The individual for whom the code had been intended had not received it because I'd put it into police hands. He wouldn't turn up, unless the information had been passed by other means; I began to wonder if, in view of recent events, the instigator of the plan would be there? Another query was whether or not the C.I.D. had cracked the code, or whether anyone in the local force had tried to decipher it. If not, I could be one of a very few people with this knowledge. I fully realised I could be barking up the wrong tree, but the possibility had to be examined—if it was true, it might answer a lot of questions. So what should I do?

I could ring Stokesley police and tell them of my beliefs, but I knew their reaction—no policeman, however courteous, likes an amateur interfering with his work or trying to tell him how to do the job. All that rubbish you read in crime novels about private eyes doing police work or helping with the enquiries, is a load of romantic nonsense. I decided not to ring them; after all, they were intelligent chaps and had probably worked it out for themselves. Anyway, it had nothing to do with me. Furthermore, I shouldn't be in possession of this numeral! Only the other night, I'd told the Special Branch that I had no further interest in the crashed Bulldog and had stressed that I couldn't remember the number. If I did ring the police, they'd begin to wonder just how involved I really was and I could land myself right in the fertiliser! The fact that the Special Branch was interested suggested that something of a very intriguing nature surrounded the aircraft and its mission and it was distinctly possible that I was in possession of some very hot information.

Undecided as to a sensible course of action, I took a walk beyond the village. I made my way to the east and climbed high on to the hills which ran behind my home. From their summit, I could look across Ryedale to the east and south, and, where there was an occasional break in the lofty heights, could view the mass of the hazy blue Pennines across to the west. I enjoyed the walk; I regularly used this route and it extended for some three miles. I always covered it briskly until the blood surged through my veins and the wind off the moors hissed among my hair. Today's keen and chilly breeze stung my cheeks and ears, and filled my lungs with pure and clean fresh air. It was a real tonic, for it was upon these heights that I liked to do my thinking. For this reason, I was here now. I wanted to think and to make decisions.

By the time I'd walked back to my cottage, I'd made up my mind. I would visit the Cleveland Tontine. I would be there between the times I'd worked out, just to see what, if anything, happened. If I had been wrong in my interpretation, it would mean using a couple of gallons of petrol and spending a couple of hours of my time, but it would also obviate the risk of making a fool of myself. If I was right, I may still learn nothing because if the police had worked out the code, they could be there too. That was something I'd have to worry about if and when they found me! I'd tell the truth if I had to; besides, I may not be recognised by the officers who attended. After all, I'd talked only to one officer at Stokesley and the two Special Branch chaps.

And if I was wrong, so what? I had nothing to lose and would enjoy the outing. I might even treat myself to an evening meal at the Tontine.

With the excitement of the unknown in my veins, I left home soon after four o'clock dressed in my second best suit, a dark one. I allowed three quarters of an hour to drive the twenty-five miles or so and pulled into the Tontine's car park five or six minutes before five o'clock. A sports car followed me in and parked next to me.

I thought nothing of it at the time, for it had been behind me for much of the journey from Thirsk. In fact, I'd overtaken it a few miles north of Thirsk and it had settled behind me for the rest of the trip. Now it eased into a parking space but I didn't take a lot of notice of the driver because I was too anxious to get inside the premises.

Having entered, I approached the receptionist.

'Has anyone left a message for Metcalfe?' I asked blithely.

She checked and said, 'No,' which gave me an excuse to remain. I would 'wait' for my non-existent message.

'I'll wait here if I may?' there were a few chairs in the reception lounge. 'Can I order afternoon tea?'

'Certainly, sir. If you take a seat I'll have it brought in for you.'

Several persons were in this part of the premises, and some were in the adjoining room talking in affable and humorous terms. I kept apart from them in order to view everyone who entered and to look over all that were present. Looking out, I noticed a woman climb from the sports car which followed me into the parking ground. She was heading for the main entrance. I watched her bathed in the glow of the floodlights, a most pleasurable sight because she was elegantly dressed, beautifully slim and blessed with a pretty face. She wore a stone coloured trouser suit and her fair hair was cut short. She'd be in her middle thirties, I guessed, and carried a suitcase in one hand with a sheepskin coat draped over the other arm.

I admired her trim figure and watched her for a few seconds until she disappeared into the building; now I waited for her to approach the reception desk. I turned in my chair. Several people were milling around the foyer and at that moment a youthful waiter appeared with a loaded tea-tray. He placed it carefully on a small table and looked at me.

'Mr Metcalfe?'

'Yes?' I smiled at him.

'Your tea, sir,' and he bowed ever so lightly as I paid and tipped him with two ten-penny pieces.

As he departed, the slim woman entered the reception area. I was moving towards my waiting tea and cakes, but her voice was pleasing and clear as she said,

'Good evening. You have a room booked for my husband and I. My name is Mrs. England.'

FIVE

Her musical voice carried to me above the hum of male chatter as she continued, 'My husband will arrive shortly.'

The receptionist was checking the bookings and smiled, 'Yes, Mrs England. Here's your key. Could you sign in please?'

The elegant woman accepted the key and began to complete the hotel register, saying, 'Can I bring the key back when I've unlocked my room? I want to surprise my husband—he doesn't know I'm ahead of him. It's a little surprise I've planned. It's our anniversary, you see. Will you do that for me? When he comes, hand him the key as if he's the first to arrive. He'll be here within the hour. You'll do that for me?'

'If you wish, Mrs England,' the receptionist smiled. 'I'll send a boy to bring back the key.'

A uniformed page appeared at the receptionist's signal and led the way, carrying Mrs England's suitcase and coat upstairs. I returned my attention to the snack I'd bought and reached for the tea-pot, only to realise that two men were standing over me. Riley and Pierce! I blinked stupidly and the total surprise must have shown on my face. They, however, showed no emotion as they pulled up two easy chairs and sat before me. I had had no idea they'd been watching; they must have been here all the time, watching me and creeping up on my blind side as all my concentration had been upon that woman.

'Mr Metcalfe! Fancy meeting you here!' Riley's pale eyes looked coldly into mine.

I managed a nervous smile as he continued, 'Isn't it strange that you should be here at this particular time? We never believed your earlier denials; so give, Mr Metcalfe. Tell us all about it. Tell us exactly what's going on and why you are *really* here.'

'I'd made a copy of the code,' I admitted.

'I did it for my own amusement, that's all. I thought I'd worked it out because it gave this date, time and place. I wanted to see what was going to happen, if anything. That's why I'm here.'

'And are you waiting for a message?' put in Pierce, speaking for the first time.

How do you explain a lie of that sort? I'd used the 'waiting for a message' technique merely to provide an excuse for being in the hotel. It's done all the time, but now it looked so bloody ominous.

I tried to explain. 'It provided me with an excuse to be here, that's all. I wanted a reason to wait until I'd tested my theory. There is no message. I'm completely alone in this.'

'Mr Metcalfe,' Riley spoke. 'I am not satisfied with your replies. I must warn you ...'

At that instant, Pierce reached over to touch his colleague's arm. A large man was the object of his immediate interest; he was at the reception desk and Riley's attention was diverted from me. They both watched the newcomer. So did I.

And furthermore, I recognised the large, dark haired man. He was Mr Reginald George MacIntyre, O.B.E., Q.P.M., one of

Her Majesty's Inspectors of Constabulary. There are only five of these men in England and Wales and one of the duties of an H.M.I. is to annually conduct a formal inspection of all police forces within the area for which he is responsible.

The duty of an H.M.I. is to report to the Home Secretary upon the efficiency or otherwise of the police forces within his jurisdiction. If he is not satisfied that any particular force is being efficiently run, he is powerful enough to secure the dismissal of a chief constable or to halt Government aid to individual forces. An H.M.I. is directly responsible to the Home Secretary who can instruct him to carry out other duties as he may from time to time direct. An H.M.I. may be allocated specific *ad hoc* assignments, for example, he may serve as a member of a committee or upon a working party, or he may act as adviser in any matter of concern to the police. He may also advise Government departments or conduct special enquiries or investigations.

This particular H.M.I. had, in the past, been the chief constable of the force which I had originally joined. When I had joined the police at the age of twenty, he'd been in charge and we had hit it off well, or as well as a chief constable can hit it off with a very junior subordinate. MacIntyre was one of the old school, a typical English gentleman of the highest calibre, trustworthy, honest and efficient, and he had taken a very close interest in all his men, myself included. He knew all 700 of us by name and had a deep interest in our joint and indeed our individual welfare, including that of our families. He visited me many times when I was stationed on a country beat, for he loved hiking and studying rural affairs. My old beat had plenty to interest him in that respect and for that reason, he knew me rather better than most. I felt I knew him both as a friend and as a boss.

I liked him and would have trusted him with my life. He was that sort of man. I'd felt his retirement rather keenly—in the police, one needs someone of authority to 'push' you gently forward upon your career and he was my pusher. And who better? Then he'd resigned some five years ago to become H.M.I. and from that time I'd hardly set eyes on him.

Until now.

I was on the point of going to greet

him when Riley put a hand on my knee. 'Don't,' was all he said.

Having recognised the newcomer, I looked at Pierce and Riley; each was watching him like a hawk. Naturally, I emulated their interest and was deeply surprised when I heard MacIntyre's booming voice say,

'My name is England. I believe you have accommodation reserved in my name.'

The page-boy must, by now, have brought back the key because, with a romantic smile on her face, the receptionist handed it to him and bade the boy carry the gentleman's case to his room.

To say I was shocked was an understatement; here was one of the men I'd most looked up to in my formative police life and he was using a false name. I was almost speechless and was so glad I hadn't introduced myself. Now, I didn't want him to see me. Here was one of the country's most powerful police officials going furtively about some underhand business. And that woman wasn't his wife, so the double falsehood was evidence of an illicit affair. I felt hurt and sadly let down. It was as if he'd openly slapped my face.

If he was behaving immorally, I could

understand the interest of these Special Branch officers. In police hierarchy, H.M.I.s are akin to royalty! That means they are beyond reproach, and if this was an illicit liaison, then security of certain police matters could be at risk. The precise risk would vary according to any specific duty upon which he was currently engaged, and also it would depend upon the character and identity of the woman. I looked around the foyer for the inevitable retinue of officials that normally accompanies an H.M.I. upon his rounds, but saw none. There is usually one, or sometimes two, staff officers plus a chauffeur, to say nothing of a gaggle of local police officers of very high rank.

MacIntyre was alone and therefore off duty. The two Special Branch men regarded all the other people in the room, but none appeared to be attached to, or interested in, the subject of our attention.

Going through my mind during those moments was the deep and vexed question as to how the aircraft with its load of £25,000, and the coded reference number, had become part of this incident. If a fellow of this stature wished to have a liaison with a woman, it is highly unlikely *he'd* go to the lengths of using vast sums of money, secret codes and long distance aircraft to achieve it. MacIntyre wouldn't have that sort of money, but someone had known of their meeting and it was someone prepared to spend £25,000 to tell another person ...

I didn't like this one bit. I turned to face my inquisitors.

'From the expression on your face just now, Mr Metcalfe, I'd say you are acquainted with that man.'

'That's true. Do you know him?'

Riley didn't answer for a few seconds, but his cold eyes blinked at me from an unsmiling face. 'His name is MacIntyre, Mr Metcalfe.'

'Then you will know his profession?' I put to him.

'We do. How is it that you know him?'

'I am an ex-police officer of the force in which this hotel is situated. Some years ago, he used to be my chief constable. Now he's the H.M.I. for this district.'

'You in the force?' Riley's eyebrows rose quickly and I could see the possibility had shaken him.

'I've been out of the job for about three months.'

'We had no idea,' he confessed.

'Didn't Stokesley Police tell you?'

'Stokesley?'

'The police there. You got my address from them.'

'Oh, that. I was given your name and address, but that's all. No one said you'd been in the job. It explains a lot—about your action at the scene of the crash, I mean.'

'I don't think it makes any difference to anything else, does it? I was able to work out the code because of my police knowledge—perhaps a policeman created it? Anyway, that's why I am here, to check if I was right for purely personal reasons. And that's the only reason I'm here.'

'What are you doing now? To earn a living?'

'Nothing. For the time being, I'm living off my savings and my returned superannuation contributions. That can't last for ever; I'll soon need a job.' I followed with a brief outline of my somewhat illogical reason for throwing up my safe job and career.

'Well, Mr Metcalfe. I think this does

alter things just a little. Tell me, how well do you know MacIntyre?'

'I don't really *know* him at all. I'm acquainted with him, having met him officially during my duties. I don't know whether he'll remember me now, because it's over five years since we spoke. I was just one of about seven hundred uniformed men under his command.'

I didn't tell them that he knew me rather better than most of his constables, but we weren't friends. Acquaintances was the correct word.

'And that woman?'

'It's not his wife. I've seen his wife at official functions' I had to admit. 'I've been racking my brains since he entered the hotel but can't recall seeing that woman before tonight. He could have re-married, I suppose; it's five years since he left our force and I know nothing of his recent private life.'

'Tell us once again how you came to be involved in this.'

I'd let my first cup of tea grow cold but poured another and sipped at it as I recounted the whole story yet again. I repeated that I'd copied the code for selfish reasons and that I was surprised the local police hadn't acted upon it. These Metropolitan detectives listened, Riley occasionally asking questions and Pierce never uttering a word.

'What do you think, Joe?' Riley asked his silent companion when I finished.

'He's telling the truth, sarge,' said Joe without qualification.

'A few minutes ago, Mr Metcalfe, I intended taking you into custody for questioning,' Riley informed me. 'I thought you had been sent to disorganise the plans of those who arranged this, but Joe's never wrong about people. He doesn't say much but he thinks a lot. I believe you are telling the truth.'

'So what happens next?' I put to him.

'We sit it out,' Riley said. 'We have booked in here indefinitely for the sole purpose of keeping an eye on MacIntyre.'

'What's he up to?'

'God knows,' Riley threw open his arms in a wild gesture. 'But it's my job to find out. What do you think?'

'You're asking me?' I laughed aloud. 'How the hell should I know? If it was a legitimate police operation there'd be none of this high finance and secrecy, would there? So it looks as though he's up to

67

something not strictly lawful. But I reckon you know that already, otherwise you'd not be here! Frankly, I'm astonished. He's one of the old school, straight as an arrow and a thorough gentleman. I can't believe he'd go bent in any way, not even to the extent of having a woman on the side.'

'A policeman's job always produces surprises, doesn't it? Anyway, it's not your problem, it's ours. What are your immediate plans, Mr Metcalfe?'

'I'm going home. I've done what I intended to do and it seems I was right. You are here to take over so I needn't worry about lack of interest by the police, nor need I concern myself any more. If there is something fishy going on, you are quite capable of coping without my interference! I'm not a copper any more and don't wish to be involved.'

'If we require a witness to prove he was here, with that woman, would you be prepared to give evidence?'

'I wouldn't have any choice, would I?'

Riley laughed. It was a cold, hard laugh and definitely humourless. 'You wouldn't. I felt I'd better remind you of the possibility. This episode may not conclude in a court, of course. If he is involved in something illegal or merely unorthodox, it could result in a tribunal or a hearing at the Home Office. If he is caught with his pants down, in a manner of speaking, he may decide to quietly resign. But all this is supposition on my part and we have a lot more questions to answer and facts to find. He may well be sleeping with his wife in spite of secret codes and crashed aircraft!'

'You've got my address?' I got up and prepared to leave.

'I'd appreciate it if you would keep this to yourself, Mr Metcalfe,' Riley rose to his feet too. 'I know we can rely on you.'

'As you wish. I'll not say a word.'

I left the hotel and made for my car. My instinctive curiosity made me take a closer look at the woman's vehicle. If MacIntyre was womanising, at least I could see what sort of car she ran! It was a dark blue M.G.B. and I mentally noted the registration number. One does this sort of thing as a policeman—looking at car registrations is an automatic reaction, just as looking at a woman's legs is natural in any red-blooded man. It was OXO 36N, and therefore so easy to memorise.

In the seclusion of my own car I jotted that number on some scrap paper and pushed it into my wallet, then drove from the Tontine's car park. I didn't take the road to Thirsk—the distance home is about the same either by Thirsk or by Stokesley, so I chose the latter, more for a change of route than for any other reason.

It was while driving through Stokesley that I noticed the lights in the police station and through the uncurtained windows could see the head and shoulders of the constable who had taken my initial report on Sunday. I pulled onto the parking space and walked in. He recognised me and led me into the general office.

'I was passing,' I said, 'so thought I'd pop in. I was curious to know if anything has developed about the crash.'

'Not a lot,' he told me. 'We haven't positively identified the pilot and the police in Buckinghamshire are making enquiries about that. We've got to find an owner for the plane too, and that isn't easy. And the Ford Escort—its number was false. It's never been issued, so we've circulated a description in the hope that one of our lads comes across it. The gunman's description has been circulated too—we're treating that as a case of robbery because he stole the money at gunpoint.'

'Did you crack the code I handed in?'

'We didn't bother to try. Our boss said if it was important, someone would come looking for it. The plane crash received enough publicity. Our C.I.D. didn't seem to think it was something they should worry about. You know how the C.I.D. react to things! If there's a chance of chalking up a detected crime, they're interested, but if it's likely to be an undetected one with no formal report of it happening, they don't want to know. Remember, we've had no official report of the loss of the money or the theft of the plane. So far as we are concerned, there is no crime as regards the aircraft and so we are treating it as a straight-forward crash. You reported a robbery from you, so we've circulated that; no one has reported losing that £25,000 into *your* possession.'

'Hasn't anyone been given copies of the coded number? Hasn't any effort been made to crack it?'

'No one's interested. One or two of our lads have had a go for their own amusement but there's been no official interest. There never is, is there? You ought to know that—when someone makes an official complaint about the loss of that code, we'll restore it to them. It's theirs, not ours. I must admit that if someone was prepared to pay £25,000 for it, it must be important and the official attitude is—why hasn't the owner shouted? The brief-case is locked in the station safe and I hold the key. I'm responsible for it until we are satisfied that a claimant is the true owner and then it will be restored. No one in any official position will admit there's a mystery, Mr Metcalfe. We have three facts—a sudden death, a plane crash and a robbery from you. We're dealing with each of those in the usual manner. When I submit my report to Divisional Headquarters, I will make reference to the code number, of course, but I can't complete the file until after the inquest.'

'When is the inquest likely to be held?'

'I don't know. It can't proceed until we trace the relatives of the pilot and get a formal identification. When that happens we can open the inquest to allow the funeral to go ahead, and then it will be adjourned until our enquiries into the crash are complete. You'll be needed at the inquest—I asked P.C. Curran to warn you.'

'He came,' I said. 'I'm still interested

in that code,' I persisted. 'Did the Special Branch ask to see it?'

'Nope,' he affirmed. 'No one's been. I was told to lock it away in the property safe until someone claimed it. It's been entered in the Found Property book in the usual way.'

This was bloody typical! No one wanted to bother themselves ... I wanted to tell this fellow about the strange affair at the Tontine only ten minutes drive away, but refrained because I'd been asked not to say anything. If the Special Branch wanted this level of the service to be told, they'd do so in their own good way.

I left the premises with a feeling of exasperation; officialdom was a fool and my frustration served only to make the mystery ring within my head. Nothing made any sense; the whole affair was so unreal and MacIntyre just wasn't the type to get involved in anything sordid. I was convinced of that. £25,000 and secret codes aren't the usual ingredients for adultery.

It would be twenty minutes after leaving Stokesley that an unsettling thought struck me. According to Riley and Pierce, and reinforced by the duty constable at Stokesley, the Special Branch men had obtained only my name and address from that police station. They'd requested nothing else and had been given nothing else. No one had asked about the code.

So how did Riley and Pierce know about England's arrival at the Tontine?

SIX

During the remaining minutes of my drive home, my mind was functioning in a typical police manner. After all, you can't forget the procedures of a decade in a matter of months. I tried to tell myself that MacIntyre's private life was his own concern; it was between himself and his conscience, but I had to admit that if I'd still been in the force, I'd have taken some official action over what I'd learned. It was true that the Special Branch fellows had the matter in hand, but their part in the affair had planted certain doubts in my mind. A deep suspicion that all was not well began to bother me.

I did wonder if I was being too

melodramatic; perhaps I was reading too much into what was probably a very straight-forward affair with a logical answer. Perhaps the plane and the money had nothing to do with MacIntyre's woman? But on the other hand, I knew I'd never rest until I had discussed my suspicions with another policeman, preferably a local man who was independent of the case and who could view it objectively. I had lots of friends in the police at York.

When I got home, I rang Gerry Sullivan. He was the sergeant in charge of the Special Branch at York and after an exchange of pleasantries, I asked if he was free tonight. I'd like to have a pint with him. He was working until midnight, but after I'd given a brief account of my reason for ringing, he said he could legitimately regard an interview with me as part of his duty. We met in the Bay Horse at Stillington which was mutually convenient and once again, I gave a full account from the moment I'd stumbled across the Bulldog, and concluded with my visit to Stokesley Police Station earlier this evening. I disobeyed the Metro. men's request because I explained to Gerry all about MacIntyre and the woman, trusting in his professional discretion.

Gerry, one of the strong silent types, listened as he puffed contentedly at his pipe and sipped from his pint of Bass-Charrington. He was a year older than I, a detective sergeant by rank and a good six feet two inches tall. His auburn hair was thinning on top and his belly was developing a beer drinker's paunch. He was good at his job and we'd been pals for years, ever since we'd met at Newby Wiske Training Centre on our initial training course.

In the time it took me to tell the complete story, we each consumed one pint and Gerry bought the second round. We were tucked nicely into a corner where normal talk was possible without the worry of being over-heard.

'I agree with your assessment of old MacIntyre,' he said. 'I'd always looked up to him. He set a fine example to others, but human nature is odd. It all goes to prove just how little we really know of each other. As I see it,' he continued, 'I've got two immediate jobs to do. One is to get the correct name of Mrs England. I can do that through her registration number, although if she's hired or borrowed that

M.G.B., I'll be knackered. If I have to ask someone else to follow up the enquiry from the hirer or the lender, it makes it all very official and takes up valuable time. Let's hope she owns it. Then I've got to check the pedigrees of those Special Branch chaps. That's enough to be going on with.'

'You don't know them?' I put the question to him.

'Nope. The names of Riley and Pierce mean nothing to me. There's no significance in that, of course, although I am acquainted with several of the Metro. S.B. lads. They do operate all over the country and it's not unusual for them to be here; they don't always acquaint us with their movements or activities.'

'Is there anything up here likely to interest them at the moment?'

'There's been a conference at Catterick Garrison,' he told me. 'It started on Monday afternoon and finished yesterday. I do know that S.B. men from all over the country were hanging around in the background, keeping an eye on things. Some of our own lads were there. It was a conference of police and army officers, with some military intelligence men there. It was connected with the troubles in Northern Ireland because some sources think the I.R.A. is using Northern Ireland as a practice ground for terrorism in England—backed by left-wing extremists. They've been debating the possible effect of those troubles upon British law and order. Several chief constables, their deputies and H.M.I.s attended.'

'Was MacIntyre among them?'

'I don't know. I wasn't there, Martin, but I can check,' and he made a note on a beer mat which he slipped into his pocket.

I next put the impossible question to him. 'What do you think he's up to?'

Gerry shrugged his shoulders. 'If it hadn't been for the £25,000 and the coded meeting place, I'd say he'd found himself a bit of crumpet. And good luck to him—she sounds a bit of all right! I can understand the Metro. Special Branch having an interest in him for that reason. If he has been knocking her off for some time, the Home Office could have found out and some of their fuddy-duddy faceless wonders may be worried about our security. It's a genuine worry, I might add. Pierce and Riley were probably sent to Catterick on observations in connection with the conference and might have been told to keep an extra eye on lover-boy. That part of it makes sense.'

'But not the cash, Gerry! And don't forget those two *knew* about the meeting place. How? That's what bothers me.'

'They must have got a copy of the code from the local police and then worked it out. You haven't thoroughly checked that angle, have you?'

'Not thoroughly. I can't do it thoroughly, can I?' But I *knew;* deep down I knew those fellows had possessed advance information. And it all meant that somehow MacIntyre *was* connected with the aircraft, and that also connected him with the gunman!

'I can check your gen tonight, Martin,' Gerry told me. 'We can make use of the computer.'

'Mrs England's car, you mean?'

He nodded. I knew that on 1st January 1974, the Police National Computer began to take on the necessary information for it to become operative on 1st January 1975. From its immense store of information, it is possible to abstract, within seconds, the name and address of the owner of any British registered motor vehicle.

In doing this, it speeds up the older system of applying to individual registration authorities at county level. The reply would furnish details of its make, colour, engine and chassis number, previous owner and, if particularly asked, it will also inform us if any vehicle is a suspect one, or stolen, or merely of long-term interest to the police.

'I'll run a check now—let's see if we can find out who she is. One point Martin—those fellows' warrant cards. Did you examine them?'

'Yes, and I did it closely. They appeared to be genuine.'

'I can check with the Yard. I've a mate on the eighth floor—that's the Special Branch offices. He might know them.'

'I suppose they could have faked those warrant cards?' I expressed this question more as a statement than a query.

'It's certainly possible. You would have no reason at the time to even suspect they might be fakes?'

'Not at the time. I'm beginning to wonder now.'

We remained in the pub long enough to sink another pint and Gerry asked if I'd care to follow him into York, a matter of eleven miles, and be present when he checked Mrs England's car. I jumped at the chance.

In his tiny office, he rang the Control Room and asked to be connected with the V.D.U. operator at our Force terminal of the Police National Computer. This done, he explained that he sought a check of the Vehicle Owners' File and he'd keep his line open to await the response. The V.D.U. operator obtained the necessary information from us, which consisted only of the car number OXO 36N, and in four seconds we had our response.

'The vehicle is an M.G.B. (G.T.) V.8,' she told us. 'It is blue in colour and the registered keeper is a Miss Alison Jean Jenkins of Carthew House, Shamblebury, Surrey. Do you want the engine and chassis numbers?'

'No thanks,' Gerry told her. 'But could you run her name through the Name Index please? Try Criminal Names first. I want to know if she has a record.'

'It won't take a minute,' our efficient operator said.

It didn't. The average time for a reply is eight seconds, and that time is barely increased even if a thousand questions are simultaneously asked.

We got ours well within the eight seconds. It told us that Alison Jean Jenkins, unmarried, born on 05.09.1945, had numerous convictions for prostitution and soliciting. She'd served one sentence of imprisonment for blackmail and made use of the following aliases: Amelia Jones, Jennifer Griffiths and Blodwen Rees, of all things. Her physical description tallied with that of the woman I'd seen and who called herself Mrs England.

Gerry wrote down the information and thanked the girl. I found the speed of the replies amazing—less than a decade ago, the police image was that of a foot-slogging or bicycling bobby saying, 'Hello, hello, hello'; today they are computerised to that extent. The age of Big Brother has almost arrived. It is closer than many of us believe.

'Well, well, well,' mused Gerry. 'Your Mrs England seems to be quite a girl. I wonder if old MacIntyre knows what he's got tangled up with?'

'She looked very smart and well-bred,' I offered, thinking of MacIntyre's own social standing.

'They always do, don't they? Now, before we do anything else, Martin, I'd better check your Special Branch friends. It seems they're onto him and in view of his lady friend's background, I'm not surprised. I think they are justified in being concerned about his activities.'

'But the money and the code!' I still couldn't believe MacIntyre was a rogue, although my faith in him was beginning to dwindle.

'Let's deal with one thing at a time. My brain doesn't operate all that quickly! We'll do a careful check and gather all our facts. Then we can see what they add up to.'

He dialled the Yard's famous telephone number and asked for the Special Branch, saying he wished to speak to Detective Inspector Megson. But Megson was out and a sergeant took the call.

'Sergeant Mortimer. Can I help you?'

'This is Detective Sergeant Sullivan, North Yorkshire Police. I'm speaking from York.'

'I'll ring back.'

This is standard procedure. It is done to ensure the caller is genuine and thus obviates the risk of passing classified information to unidentified callers. A minute later, the phone rang and Gerry answered it.

'I'm checking on two men who claim to be Special Branch officers of your Force. They produced Metro. warrant cards, but in view of some special circumstances, I felt I'd better verify their names.'

'Go ahead,' his London accent was very pronounced and I could hear his voice if I strained my ears. 'Who are they?'

'Riley and Pierce. Detective Sergeant and Detective Constable respectively.'

'We have two men of that name, sergeant. They are engaged on an enquiry in your part of the country. Can you describe them?'

'No, but my mate can. I'll put him on.'

I took the phone.

'Hello,' I said.

'Who's that?'

'My name is Metcalfe,' I told him. 'Riley is in his middle thirties, over six feet tall and very slim. He's got sharp features, bushy dark hair and noticeably uneven teeth. His mate, Pierce, is tall too but stouter. His hair is fairer and it is thin and very straight. He hardly ever says a word.'

'Tweeldedum and Tweedledee!' laughed Mortimer. 'It's them all right.'

'I'll hand you back to Sergeant Sullivan.'

Gerry took the phone again. 'Can I ask what they are doing up here?'

'I'm not allowed to explain over the public telephone system, Mr Sullivan, but I am sure that Riley and Pierce will be only too pleased to put you in the picture if you care to contact them. You'll need proof of your identify, of course. They are staying at the Cleveland Tontine Hotel. Do you know it? It's near a small town called Stokesley.'

'I know it,' Gerry said.

'Well, is that all?' I heard Mortimer ask.

'Yes thanks. It'll do for the time being.'

'I'm glad to be of help. Goodbye.'

As he put down the handset, Gerry pursed his lips. 'You heard all that? It would seem that your little mystery is in good hands, Martin. I'll bet our C.I.D. bosses at Headquarters are in the picture. Clearly old MacIntyre is up to his bloody neck in some form of jiggery-pokery and they've rumbled him. The Home Office will have used Metro. lads in case he recognised any local ones.'

'That still doesn't explain the money, the plane, the code or the gunman!' I insisted. Those features of the affair bothered me.

Had it not been for them, I'd have gone along with Gerry's interpretation but there were too many unanswered questions.

Gerry could see I was dissatisfied. 'I'll do a spot of private snooping,' he promised. 'I must admit my theory does have weaknesses, but it's out of our hands. It's no concern of ours, and my advice is to forget all about it. Now, let's get back to your personal problems—have you traced that grey saloon?'

It was after ten-thirty when I left him to drive the twenty miles home. I slept well and rose soon after eight to make my customary breakfast of toast, marmalade and coffee. Today was Friday when all the local papers arrived and this meant a mammoth reading session. There was the one from my childhood area, one from Julie's home area and another from the district in which I now lived. Also on Fridays, I had developed the habit of touring the local scrap yards in the hope that I'd find a discarded grey saloon of some sort, one from which I would take paint samples to have checked against the deposits which I'd salvaged from my wrecked vehicle. I'd drawn a mighty blank so far, but took the attitude that one day

I'd hit the jackpot. That way, there was always hope.

I began my reading session with the *Yorkshire Post* and it was two items on the front page which caught my eye. One was a murder, the other a vice raid.

There was a photograph of the murdered man and I knew immediately that he was the fellow who'd relieved me of that £25,000! The other piece of news said that the Dales home of Mr Reginald George MacIntyre O.B.E., Q.P.M., one of Her Majesty's Inspectors of Constabulary had been entered by police who were anxious to interview him. He was missing from home, said the report, and it was wished to speak to him about a large number of pornographic books which had been found in the outbuildings.

SEVEN

It was possible that I was one of the few persons, maybe the only one, who was able to prove the link between the two reports. On that fact alone, MacIntyre seemed to be deeply implicated and echoes of past headlines about police corruption and their involvement in criminal affairs came to mind as I read the stories.

The press made no suggestion that the two events were in any way related.

The murder victim had been identified as Paul Francis Thompson, a waiter; he was twenty-nine years old and had been shot through the head. His body had been dumped over the cliffs at Boulby which lies between Saltburn and Whitby, and had apparently been there for two or three days. Its discovery was by a lucky chance; the occupants of a passing fishing coble had spotted it in the rocky shallows beneath the cliff.

No weapon had been found and no motive disclosed. Thompson's body had been identified through his criminal record, his fingerprints had clinched the matter and his wife had then been notified. The report said the police wanted to trace his past movements and they were appealing for witnesses. The press photograph was a copy of the official police mug-shot—anyone could see that! Fortunately, the likeness was good and I recognised him instantly; he must have been through police hands fairly recently.

With a feeling of intense excitement, I turned to the item about MacIntyre. It occupied the same page but was restricted to a tiny paragraph near the bottom. It was careful not to openly say he was wanted in connection with the obscene literature. The house had been searched, so the report would have us believe, because they were worried about him. The house had been unoccupied at the time of the search and his wife had been traced to her sister's home in West Yorkshire. The fact that dirty books had been traced during the search was made to appear incidental, but this was the journalist's way of avoiding libel. You state facts without making accusations and let the reader draw his own conclusions.

It occurred to me that there must have been a leak to the press. A careless member of the raiding party had probably said just a little too much when too many ears were flapping. In a case of alleged publication of indecent matter, the details aren't usually published until after the court hearing, but in this case the official position of the suspect gave valuable import to the story. It could be implied from the paragraphs that the police were seeking MacIntyre to charge him under the Obscene Publication Act, and I knew where he was. Furthermore, I knew of his link with the murder and my past respect for R.G. MacIntyre, Q.P.M. was now at a very low ebb.

I couldn't sit this one out. I couldn't pretend that it had nothing to do with me. I couldn't close my eyes to this because the whole affair had suddenly exploded into something almost incredible and all my loyalties must be discarded as I took steps to perform my public duty.

I knew that I had the power, even as a civilian, to arrest MacIntyre on suspicion of murder for the events of the past few days had provided sufficient evidence of what the law terms 'reasonable suspicion that he had committed an arrestable offence', i.e. the murder. Even if he hadn't committed it, it seemed he was deeply implicated. There is an additional power of arrest—any person, police or civilian, has the power to arrest anyone whom he finds *in the act* of committing an arrestable offence. The precise power which I could exercise was 'Where an arrestable offence had been committed, any person may arrest anyone whom he, with reasonable cause, suspects to be guilty of it.' That was my power—I'd remembered it from my training school days. The police have many additional powers, but this was enough for me. It isn't a civilian's *duty* to effect these arrests but he does have the power should he ever have cause to use it. You might find someone breaking into your house or stealing your wallet—thus you can arrest him.

This meant I could dash over to the Tontine and arrest old MacIntyre, but it isn't my job any more. I'd be over-stepping my public responsibility and the correct procedure in this case was to ring the police.

I rang the Detective Chief Superintendent at my old Headquarters, but he'd left the premises. It seemed that the two Special Branch detectives resident at the Tontine had revealed MacIntyre's whereabouts, and he was already in custody. For the moment, he was detained in Stokesley Police Station.

I asked the policeman to whom I was speaking if he knew of the connection with the Boulby murder and he said no. After a brief explanation from me, he said he'd immediately contact the Detective Chief Superintendent, who was at Stokesley, and ask him to ring me about it.

Detective Chief Superintendent Bird rang within ten minutes.

'I want a word with you, young man,' he said. 'I'm at Stokesley Police Station but will be leaving for Richmond with our prisoner in about ten minutes. Give me a quick outline of what you've got to tell me.'

I told him and he said, 'Right. I must talk to you. When will it be convenient?'

'I'm free all day.' I decided at that instant to forgo today's hunt for grey saloons. Julie would understand—any policeman's wife (or widow) would understand because the job always comes first.

'I expect to be at Richmond most of the day with this one,' Bird explained. 'Is it too much to expect you to drive over? It would help considerably if you could. I need every man I've got and you live too far away from here for me to pop over. I'd like a personal chat, Mr Metcalfe. We will reimburse your petrol and you might even get a meal thrown in!'

'I'll set off immediately, sir.' I still called him 'sir', an automatic reaction when addressing a man of senior rank.

'It will take me about an hour—it's forty miles from my home.'

'Ask for me in person when you arrive. I'll be there before you,' and Bird slammed down the phone. I made sure I took all my notes, including those I'd made last night during the telephone conversation with Mortimer and not forgetting the computer's responses. It was twenty minutes to ten when I arrived at Richmond Police Station.

This is the Divisional Headquarters for a large tract of police area including the Stokesley district. That's why MacIntyre was brought here—Stokesley was merely a sectional station and therefore hardly able to cope with cases of this nature. Those of you who know Yorkshire's Richmond will take pride in its mellow stone beauty, its idyllic setting on the River Swale, its ancient and stirring history and its sturdy no-nonsense populace. In and around this town have lived generations of dalesmen, all hard-working, honest and God-fearing, and they live there to this day. It was here, high on Richmond Hill, that they built the impressive new police station. Richmond Hill, of course, is framed in the song 'Sweet Lass of Richmond Hill', written by Leonard MacNally as a love song to Frances I'Anson, a maid of this beautiful old town.

I'd been there many times, of course. In fact, my surname is an old Dales name and the Metcalfes have occupied the Yorkshire Dales since the beginnings of time and for that reason, I have always experienced a certain affinity with the folk who live there, although I have never traced my family tree to see if I had any direct relatives or ancestors in the Richmond area. I had been born nearer the coast, but when I had nothing to do, I'd begin the search for my past relatives ...

I parked in the street outside the Fire Station because the police office car-park was packed with cars, a sure indication that something important was afoot. I recognised the Chief Constable's car and those of several other high-ranking officers. The arrest of an H.M.I. was bound to guarantee the arrival of high officials, but in the long term it must surely cast serious doubts on the integrity of the entire British police service. The press, however, was conspicuous by its absence and doubtless the news of his arrest had been kept from them. They'd be up in the dales, scouring the countryside near his home!

I walked in and waited at the enquiry counter.

'Good morning, Alan,' I smiled at the duty constable. 'Is Detective Chief Superintendent Bird in please?'

'Hello, Martin! It's been a long time since we saw you. I was sorry to hear about your family. What a bloody awful thing to happen.'

'Thanks for your sympathy,' I had known Alan for years and had frequently called in this station in the course of my duty.

'You're out of the force now, eh? Resigned. I saw it on General Orders ...'

'Yes, I couldn't see the point of staying in. But it's Mr Bird ...'

I had to cut him short and I think he saw my growing impatience.

'Mr Bird is very busy, Martin, far too busy to see anyone right now. Can I help?'

'No, it's got to be him, Alan. That's why I'm here. I have an appointment with him. It's connected with MacIntyre.'

'Oh!' his expression sought an explanation, but I could offer none. 'I'll buzz him.'

A cadet took me upstairs to the C.I.D. offices and I was shown in. A sea of pink faces filled the large room and among them I recognised Riley and Pierce. I noticed the present Chief Constable and many other faces, some known but many unknown.

Bird came forward as a strange silence filled the room; I was an intruder in their midst. Everyone ceased their chatter as the Detective Chief Superintendent hailed me.

'Come in, Mr Metcalfe. Gentlemen, this is Martin Metcalfe, an ex-member of our force. Many of you will know him, I'm sure. He is a material witness in this case and has some valuable information for us.'

There was a buzz of chatter and I was ushered through that room, across the corridor and into the Detective Superintendent's office. This was the office of the Divisional chief of C.I.D. who carried the rank of Superintendent, but who came under the supervision of Mr Bird who was based at Headquarters. The Chief Constable, Riley and another man came with us and we all found chairs in the somewhat cramped space. The rest of the team were not allowed to hear my words and all the doors were closed.

Bird addressed me.

'I've heard a little of your involvement, Mr Metcalfe. Detective Sergeant Riley has been telling me. This is Mr Herriott from the Security Service,' he introduced the tall, clean cut stranger, a man in his late forties. We shook hands. I was then introduced to the Chief Constable.

He spoke to me. 'I'd like to hear your story, Mr Metcalfe. Every detail please.' This was the man who'd taken over that appointment from MacIntyre upon his retirement. I'd never met him until now, but had heard much; it seems he was a strict disciplinarian, as hard as nails, but an ideal man to lead this huge force.

I'd lost count of the number of times I'd related my story, but once more gave a full account and provided the punchline by relating my shock at seeing those two items in today's paper. The Chief's face paled a little. I could imagine the nationwide horror that would arise if my suspicions were true, and his life would be uncomfortable for some time afterwards.

The Home Office would want a report about the matter.

'The man who relieved you of the cash,' Riley's cockney accent sounded strange in these hills. 'Can you be sure from the press photograph that it is one and the same person?'

'As sure as humanly possible, Mr Riley. If I could be allowed to view the body, I would be completely certain, one way or the other.'

'We can arrange that,' offered Detective Chief Superintendent Bird.

Riley spoke rapidly and with a trace of nervous excitement. 'I think Mr Herriott will agree that we have no need to concern ourselves with that murder, gentlemen. We have no reason to suspect that MacIntyre is in any way involved in that death. He's barely been out of our sight during the past week.'

Herriott was nodding furiously.

The Chief Constable, however, disagreed. 'Cleveland Police are investigating the murder because the body was found in their area, and it would be grossly wrong of us to keep this information from them. We must also concern ourselves in it, in view of the developments described by Mr Metcalfe. We cannot ignore the fact that the man who removed the cash from Mr Metcalfe and who handed to him the code which revealed Mr MacIntyre's whereabouts, has been found shot and dumped over a cliff. The matter must be investigated thoroughly.'

Riley wanted to speak in reply and I saw Herriott give him a swift nod, the signal to go ahead.

'It's time for us to be completely frank,' he began. 'I am going to give you information which is of the utmost secrecy. I do so with Mr Herriott's approval, and with the object of preventing Mr Metcalfe stirring up too much trouble and dirty mud. It is therefore necessary that he also hears what I have to say.'

Herriott gave another nod of approval.

'The dead man, Thompson, was a small-time crook, sir,' he addressed himself to the Chief Constable. 'He was used by the Security Service as a tool in a very necessary plot. It is because of that plot—a plot about which none of you were told—that we are here today. It cost £25,000 to make use of Thompson's services, expertise and contacts, and to buy his secrecy. With regard to his death, it is

99

pretty clear that someone knew that he was loaded with lovely money in crisp new notes—a fortune in hard cash. I think he was killed for that money, sir; I do not think Mr MacIntyre is in any way involved in his murder. Thompson was a rogue—he's received his just desserts. I have no idea who killed him and I feel it is of no concern to us.'

'*You* used him?' I stared at Riley and Herriott. 'Why?'

'Mr Herriott will explain. It will be a revelation to you, Chief Constable, and to you, Mr Bird. I must remind each of you of the declaration of secrecy you signed upon joining the police—and that includes you, Mr Metcalfe. Your declaration remains binding. No one must divulge a word of this and it is because of Mr Metcalfe's unwitting involvement, and his past service in the police, that we may put all of you in the picture.'

'Get on with it!' snapped the Chief Constable. 'Metcalfe knows his responsibilities.'

Herriott began.

'Mr MacIntyre is, as you all know, the past chief constable of a very efficient local force—this one, in fact. He retired to accept the appointment of Her Majesty's Inspector of Constabulary when the post was offered to him by the Home Office. That was five years ago. Since that time, the Security Service has had a very sound reason for suspecting that he was in league with certain subversive elements of our society whose ultimate aim is to disrupt the smooth running of this country. In short, it was believed that he had become a secret member of a left-wing subversive group or at least had become a fellow traveller.'

'An H.M.I. doing that?' I gasped. God! This fellow's life *was* full of surprises.

'Yes, and think of the terrible implications. He has access to police records all over the country; he serves on committees, many of them secret and concerned with national security, and on top of that, he is a direct link between the Home Office and the police authorities. He helps to frame the national police policy. He is therefore a very powerful and important man, and an ideal recruit for extremists. In this case, they succeeded in getting him into their net. They have caught a very big fish indeed.'

I stared at Riley as Herriott continued, 'The Security Service thought it necessary to put the Metropolitan Police Special Branch in the picture and the two services have since observed and recorded his activities. We have watched him closely over the last two years gathering evidence to confirm our suspicions. It was not possible to acquaint chief constables with the nature of our work because many of them are close personal friends of Mr MacIntyre. We could not risk our activities becoming known to him. Finally, we had to be completely sure of our facts before taking any sort of action.'

Herriott paused to let the full import of his words sink in.

'Today we have sufficient information to justify our concern, but even so we do not have the sort of evidence needed to prove a criminal case in court. To our knowledge, he has committed no breach of the Official Secrets Act and no other criminal offence, so we cannot proceed against him through the normal processes of law. To prosecute him, or to have him dismissed from his post would require irrefutable factual evidence and first-rate witnesses. We could not risk a failure, nor could we risk the alarming disclosures that a public hearing would produce. So we created a plot. We had no real alternative; our mission is to compel him to resign from his position.'

'So you blackmailed him?' I used the word deliberately.

'Yes, we did. The Security Service has to resort to some pretty crude and cruel tactics at times, Mr Metcalfe. We rigged up a plot to blackmail him and to frame him for a criminal offence. Thompson, the deceased, was paid £25,000 to secure the services of a prostitute who was willing, if necessary, to testify in any court or at any hearing, of her liaison with him. We used the oldest method of blackmail—the illicit and adulterous meeting in an hotel. We had to make sure the room was booked in false names; we knew he was using the name "England" for some of his enterprises, and Thompson did the rest. The prostitute was to be paid by him for her services—Thompson was left to arrange all that. He was well paid for his part in the operation—we use only the best, and we used agents outside the Service to eradicate the risk of official censure. Neither Thompson nor the woman knew of the real reason behind their work. Once Thompson had fixed everything, he told us, in code, of the date, time and place. Unfortunately, the aircraft crash complicated everything. We overcame that, thanks to Mr Metcalfe's honesty. Mrs England was armed and she kept MacIntyre in that hotel room until we raided the place and "found" them together.

'In the time he was away from home, we planted the dirty books and hey presto, we have one very blackened character. When the Home Office receives our report, they will ask him to resign. The alternative will be a court appearance, but not one connected with his political beliefs. He will be charged under the Obscene Publications Act, and that's a guarantee of publicity. If he resigns, he will leave his career without a public stain upon his character. If he refuses to resign, we can prove our allegations up to the hilt, including his association with a convicted prostitute, and he'll have to answer our allegations in open court. The choice is his. Either way, we get rid of him and that's vital for police security.'

'It's a dirty way of doing it,' I spoke quietly.

'It's a dirty world, Mr Metcalfe, and in this case the end justifies the means,' smiled Mr Herriott.

EIGHT

My evidence was therefore a vital part of the operation and I was interviewed by Detective Chief Superintendent Bird. He personally took a lengthy written statement from me, an indication of the importance of this arrest and during the interview the seized pornographic books arrived. A police van had ferried them from Startforth Police Station where they'd been lodged overnight, and upon Bird's instructions two detectives carried them into the billiard room. For them, this was a genuine enquiry and they knew nothing of the drama behind it. A full list of the books, including publishers, authors and titles would be made, for it is not illegal merely to possess pornographic literature. The offence arises when a person *publishes* obscene articles, whether for gain or not, and if they possess such articles *for gain*. I knew that the term 'publishers' includes distributing, circulating, selling, letting on hire, giving, tendering or offering for sale or let on hire, so presumably the evidence against MacIntyre would include proof of his 'publication for gain' or his 'possession for gain'. These boys would have thought of all the legal loopholes and they'd have been sealed before poor old MacIntyre could use them. He wouldn't have a cat-in-hell's chance of proving his innocence.

I knew of no power to arrest him for this alleged offence so they must have trumped up another charge to give them power to detain him. They would have planted a drug or 'stolen' object in either his hotel room, car or home to provide the necessary 'holding' charge.

Herriott, Riley and the Chief Constable were in the room as Bird questioned me and each of them occasionally addressed queries to me, the answers of which were incorporated in my statement. It was eleven o'clock when I finished; someone rustled up a cup of coffee for us and all but Mr Bird vanished into the Chief Superintendent's office for theirs. Bird stayed with me to round off the statement. He said that Cleveland Police would want me to have a look at their murdered man because they were anxious to trace his movements. I'd have to positively identify him as the man who took the cash. Bird rang their Murder Room which had been established at Loftus Police Station. Detective Chief Superintendent Senior was in charge.

'Alf?' Bird said into the phone. 'This is Dicky Bird. I'm speaking from Richmond. It's to do with that murder of yours, at Boulby. I've a young fellow here by the name of Metcalfe who's had recent contact with somebody he thinks is your victim. He'll explain it all if you want, but he'll have to view the corpse, to decide if it is the bloke in question.'

I couldn't hear the reply, but after putting down the phone, Bird addressed me.

'Can you drive over to Loftus? Be there for two o'clock and ask for Detective Chief Superintendent Senior. He's expecting you. It'll take an hour and a half from here, but that will allow you time for lunch. He'll show you the body and if it is your gunman, he'll want a statement of identification from you.'

'How much am I allowed to divulge?' Clearly, I could not acquaint Cleveland Police with the connection between the killing and MacIntyre.

'Take it from where you found the plane to the point where you had to hand over the money at gunpoint. You can mention the brief-case and its contents, but leave it at that. You know nothing more. If Senior wants to know more—as he will because he'll wonder how I'm involved in your story—tell him to ring me. I'll be here most of the day.'

'Yes, sir.'

'I'll tell Herriott what we've done. Now, petrol. You've already driven a hell of a long way for our benefit, so take this.'

He pushed a five pound note into my hands but I made a feeble effort to decline it.

'Take it, lad! I can recoup it through expenses. You've earned it—there'll be enough to buy a meal too.'

I accepted and left the office. Bird followed me out and went along the corridor to join the Chief Constable and the others, saying his next job was a long talk with MacIntyre.

I arrived at Loftus Police Station at

two o'clock to find Senior waiting and with no more ado, he drove me to the mortuary. The body was undoubtedly that of the man I'd seen last Sunday. Having made my formal identification, I would have to put that fact into yet another written statement and would need to detail our confrontation. Senior wanted to know more about me and my involvement and, as we stood over Thompson's body, I told him in the restricted terms outlined at Richmond.

'Let's consider the brief-case he carried,' Detective Superintendent Senior began. 'Could you identify it if we traced it?'

'It's the same as the one now at Stokesley,' I said. 'I couldn't positively identify it against others of the same style, except that it has the initials "P.B.G." on the lid.'

'We haven't found it yet,' Senior said. 'But of course we haven't had any reason to look for it until now. We've searched his house and didn't find that sort of cash. We'll certainly look into his murder from this new angle. It seems we now have a motive.'

'Someone must have known about his windfall,' I heard myself say. 'And they've decided it was worth killing him for.'

'We'll pursue that one for now, but tell me, what do you think the Bulldog was up to?'

'I don't know,' I shook my head. 'Stokesley Police have all the details of the crash and Detective Chief Superintendent Bird may be able to help you further. He suggested you contact him in person if you need further enlightenment.'

'That means there is summat behind all this, Mr Metcalfe. Can you tell me more about the dead chap?'

'I've never clapped eyes on him until last Sunday, sir.'

'He's a rogue, a professional criminal who's a mercenary character and who'd undertake most jobs, legal or otherwise, if the money was right. For the past few weeks he's been a waiter, God knows why.'

'Where, sir.'

'At a country hotel near Stokesley. It's the Cleveland Tontine—do you know it?'

'I do,' I said without elaboration.

'He wouldn't take a job of any sort, let alone become a waiter unless he had a very good reason. We've checked with the manager and he wasn't seen there after one o'clock on Sunday afternoon. That was the last time he was seen alive—until you handed him £25,000!'

'I didn't kill him!' I cried.

'I don't think you did, but someone's got £25,000 for their trouble, haven't they? We'll have to trace your movements since then, I'm afraid. I've got to eliminate you from the enquiry. You see, *you* knew he had the cash, and you are out of work. That gives you a motive!'

'I think I can account for most of my time since then,' I was thinking about my visits to the police, the phone calls I'd made and the time spent in the village. I felt safe enough. 'Is he married?' I asked.

'Yes. He's got a nice little wife and two bairns. His home is at Stockton-on-Tees and it's a nice semi, very well furnished and clean. He lived well, make no mistake about it, even though he was a criminal. His wife has been interviewed and can't throw any light on the killing. He wasn't in the habit of talking to her about his work.'

'It will obviously help if you find the brief-case that contained the cash, and the Ford Escort with the false plates. They must be somewhere and the cash was all in new notes, sir. Then there's the dead pilot ...'

'All right, all right. I've got enough leads for now! You've been a great help. I'll bet you miss this job, don't you?'

'I do—and don't mind admitting it.'

'Why not rejoin? They'd have you back, surely?'

'I'm too old really and besides, I don't like admitting that I was wrong—even if I was! I know I was a bloody fool to chuck it in, but it's too late now. I've made the proverbial bed and I'll have to lie on it.'

'I'll record your address from the statement you've got to make because I might want more information from you, Mr Metcalfe. I've enough to be going on with. Come along, let's get out of this bloody place and back to the office.'

He drove me back to the police station where I wrote out my statement and signed it. He asked me to account for my whereabouts after handing over the money and having provided it, he said he'd check it out. After all, I was a bloody good suspect—and one with a motive.

'I may need you for the inquest,' he said before I left. 'You were the last to see him alive.'

'I realise that, sir. I'll come if you want me.'

'Thanks—and thanks for volunteering this information.'

It was half-past three when I left Loftus Police Station. As I drove from its car-park, a white mini-car with a pretty, dark haired girl at the wheel, entered and jerked to a halt. As I prepared to enter the main road, I heard her get out and say to two children in the back, 'Wait here. I won't be long,' before approaching the front door. I caught a glimpse of her—a tall girl about twenty-five years old with very good legs and a slender figure. Her tweed coat was open down the front as she hurried inside.

I got home at quarter to five, having driven well over a hundred miles. I was tired, but made myself a tea of scrambled eggs on toast, followed by tinned pears and cream. I had no plans for the evening, and decided to pop out for my customary couple of pints about nine o'clock. In the meantime, there was a lot of housework to be done. I hadn't hoovered the living room for a week and the whole house needed a good dusting and tidy-up. It was while going about those chores that the phone rang. The effort of cleaning up had made me perspire and I had to wipe my hands before picking up the phone.

'Metcalfe,' I sat in the window seat to answer it.

'Hello?' said a woman's voice, apparently some distance away.

'Hello. This is Martin Metcalfe speaking,' I increased the volume of my voice, not recognising that of my caller.

She was hesitant and when I prompted her she began, 'My name is Barbara Thompson. I'd like to speak to you, urgently.'

'Now?' I suggested.

'Not on the telephone,' she said briskly. 'I'd like to meet you somewhere.'

'What about?' I was interested to say the least, particularly as I didn't know the woman.

'My husband,' she stifled a sob but it didn't escape me. 'He was killed and the police said that you were the last person to see him alive. I just wanted to talk to you about it.'

That Mrs Thompson? 'The police have all the details,' I reminded her, speaking gently. 'Didn't they tell you?'

There was a long pause; I knew she was

weeping so I waited in silence.

'They told me quite a lot, but I wanted someone to help me ...' and her voice trailed away.

'But you don't know me!'

'No, but ...'

'Go on,' I encouraged her to continue, even though there was little I could do. Talking might help her.

'You were the last to see him alive. Please let me talk to you.'

'If I can be of any help, I'll be only too pleased. Shall I drive over?'

'No, I'll come to you.'

'You live in Stockton, don't you? It's an awful long way—could we meet somewhere midway? Say Guisborough? Would the Moorcock Inn be suitable? It's as near equi-distant as dammit.'

'It's very kind of you. I can get there quite easily.'

'Good, then it's a date,' I affirmed. 'I'll wait in the car park in my car,' and we exchanged registration numbers and agreed on eight o'clock. Quite frankly, I was sick of tearing about the countryside but never could resist a pretty woman, still less a woman in distress. I wondered if she was pretty. She had an attractive voice, but that meant nothing. I'd met some right old hags with lovely voices.

By eight o'clock I was in the car-park. The Moorcock is a comparatively new inn on the outskirts of Guisborough and soon a young woman approached my car. I hadn't seen Mrs Thompson arrive but recognised the approaching person as the one with the white mini-car, the girl who'd gone into Loftus Police Station as I was leaving this afternoon. She wore the same tweed coat and hesitated before finally coming to my car. Sensing her nervousness, I opened the door and asked, 'Mrs Thompson?'

'Yes?' she was nervous; it was only to be expected and she looked most miserable and unhappy.

'Martin Metcalfe,' I climbed out and locked the doors, then faced her. She was close to tears and her dark eyes were holding them back with a commendable effort so I broke the ice by holding out my hand. She shook it delicately and managed a gentle smile.

'I hope you don't think I'm being silly,' she began.

'I won't know until you've told me why you are here,' I hoped to conquer her nervousness. 'Anyway, let's go inside and

116

I'll buy you a drink.'

She said she'd love one and I took her into a cosy corner; I ordered a pint of bitter and she requested a small lager. We made polite conversation about the inn and the weather and she seemed loath to come to the point. I had to practically force her to tell me why she'd dragged herself out of the house to meet a complete stranger.

Eventually she tackled the problem by saying, 'Loftus Police gave me your address.'

'I guessed they had!' I smiled.

'They said you were the last to see him alive.'

'Not quite the last,' I corrected her. 'I didn't harm him, Mrs Thompson. Someone else must have seen him after me, and the police haven't traced that person. I am just an innocent bystander in the affair.'

'That's what the police told me. They said you had nothing to do with his death, and that's why I wanted to see you, Mr Metcalfe. I'm sure you are not guilty—I wouldn't have come to you otherwise.'

'Go on.'

She was growing more confident and began to remove her overcoat. I helped and she laid it across a spare seat. Beneath she wore a close fitting woollen dress which revealed a good figure with small, but firm breasts.

'I'd like you to tell me exactly what happened,' she sounded like a police officer!

'Didn't they tell you?'

'Yes, but very briefly. He is—er, was—my husband, but until this afternoon, I knew nothing about the aircraft or the £25,000. I want to know what he was mixed up in, Mr Metcalfe. Can you tell me? The police won't reveal anything.'

I told her how I chanced upon the crashed aircraft, rescued the cash and had been confronted by her husband. I mentioned the Ford Escort with false plates, the gun, his matching brief-case and the coded number. During my account, I took great pains to convince her that my involvement was entirely innocent and accidental, and I mentioned Julie's death to explain my wanderings across those isolated and wintry heights. Mrs Thompson listened intently, her dark eyes occasionally moist and her face sad. Upon completion of my tale, during which I had omitted all reference to MacIntyre, I waited for her reaction.

'I was hoping you might tell me exactly what he was doing, Mr Metcalfe. I want to know what he was mixed up in, and how deeply he was involved with the aircraft and its mission. I thought you might be one of his partners or something, or that you knew what was going on. You can tell me, you know. I can keep a secret.'

'Mrs Thompson. I'd never seen him before, nor am I involved in any way whatever. That's the truth. You *do* know how he earned his living?'

'Yes. He was a criminal, Mr Metcalfe, and I knew it. I knew that before I married him. His record looks bad on paper but the truth is he was a kind, generous and loving person. He never hurt anyone, Mr Metcalfe, not physically. He stole from the rich and from others who preyed on weaker persons. He would blackmail those who had blackmailed others and he gave a lot of his money to charities, particularly to the thalidomide children. I loved him. He was a good man, Mr Metcalfe,' and she began to cry.

I didn't interrupt her tears and she soon dried them.

'He was a sort of modern Robin Hood?' I smiled. 'Or Simon Templar?'

'Yes. He loved us and kept us well provided for. He would undertake "jobs" as he called them, for other people or organisations. They would commission him to commit burglaries, for example, or get information for them. He'd break into houses to recover incriminating photographs or documents from blackmailers and restore them to his clients, the victims. That was the sort of work he did.'

'And people employed him to do that?'

'Yes, he was a freelance, Mr Metcalfe and he rarely stole for himself. He did make use of others from time to time—I thought you might be one of his helpers—but he never told me precisely the job he was doing at any one time. I couldn't unwittingly let something slip, but sometimes he did talk about smaller aspects of his work. He'd mention minor points that worried him, without giving too much away. He'd often talk in bed, when we were alone and quiet.'

'And he said something about this one, eh?'

She nodded and took a sip from her glass. 'He didn't tell me what it was—he

120

never did. But he did say he didn't like it. It wasn't often he said that because he regarded every new job as a challenge. He would turn down jobs he didn't like because he had his own code of rules about which he accepted and which he didn't.'

'Then why did he accept this one?'

'For the money. He said it would pay enough to give us our independence. It would provide us with the capital to start a small legitimate business. That's what he always wanted. It was his ambition.'

'Did he say how much the job would be worth?'

'He said it might pay as much as £20,000.'

It didn't need an accountant to work out that, from the £25,000 received from the pilot, he'd have to pay the prostitute and any others who helped, but the balance would be his. And now he was dead with that huge sum unaccounted for. I began to wonder whether I had contributed to his death. My innocent intervention might have cost him his life, but was that possible? This was an 'official' job backed by the Home Office and the Security Service. They wouldn't resort to murder! Or would they?

'What is it that bothers you so much? You haven't told me,' I put the question gently.

'It was something he said before he left to do the job. He repeated the fact that he didn't like this one. It stank, he said. I asked him why he was so bothered about it and I'll always remember his words. He said, "Because I'm doing this one for the bloody cops! Imagine that—me being paid by the cops to do a blackmailing job". He laughed as he said it, but I knew he wasn't too happy, Mr Metcalfe. And now he's dead. I think the police killed him—they must have, mustn't they? If he was doing a rotten job in their pay, a job that could pay as much as £20,000 he'd know too much to be allowed to live, wouldn't he? But I can't go to them, can I? I can't accuse the police of killing him because they'll just cover it all up, won't they? I just wanted to know if you knew anything about the job ... I wanted help, Mr Metcalfe. Somebody's got to help me find the truth, haven't they? That's all I want. I can't get him back but I must know the truth ...'

And she burst into a flood of tears.

NINE

'He would know too much to be allowed to live'. From all she had told me, those words were the most significant. They reinforced my belief that MacIntyre was the centrepiece of a very strange business and I told myself that the coincidence of Thompson being murdered by persons outside the conspiracy was just too great to be acceptable. If anyone had wanted him dead, it would be the conspirators. That was simple, straightforward logic.

At Richmond Police Station, they'd dismissed Thompson's death as if it was totally unconnected with the MacIntyre affair. They'd written it off, saying it must have been someone after the money. It probably was—but there was more to it, I was sure. Like the others, I'd accepted it as such, content to let it be investigated by Cleveland Police who knew nothing of the Bulldog's crash and Thompson's role in it. To get a true picture of the mystery, I tried to put myself in the position of a total outsider. I imagined I was a high-ranking detective who'd been brought in to investigate the entire incident and who'd been put in full possession of all the facts. Taking everything into consideration, the murder *had* to be connected with the aircraft and therefore linked with MacIntyre's troubles. And now Mrs Thompson had voiced her suspicions. Did she know more? Had her buccaneer husband learned too much about this job?

I knew virtually nothing about him but wondered if he had carried out his own investigation into those who had commissioned this blackmail? If so, what had he discovered?

The more I thought about the whole unsavoury business, the more unsettled I became, and my lone brooding was halted when Mrs Thompson returned from the ladies. She had powdered her face but her eyes still bore signs of her recent distress. She sat beside me and attempted a brave smile.

'How about another drink?' I suggested.

She said she'd like one but only one. She'd have to be going soon because a neighbour was looking after the children, so I obtained another small lager and a pint for myself.

'Mrs Thompson,' I said. 'Although you know nothing about me, you have asked me to help in a matter that could be most explosive.'

'I'm sorry. I didn't really mean to let go like that, and I had no wish to impose my troubles on you. Forget all that I asked, please. I had no right to ask you. I really came because you were the last person to see Paul. The police said you spoke to him—I thought you might throw some light on ... well, on everything.'

'I'm sorry, but I am merely an outsider. Nonetheless, I am willing to help if you want, but I must be honest with you. There is something you ought to know about me, and it is that I was a policeman myself until only three months ago.'

Her face revealed the dismay she must have experienced at that moment, so I strove to put her at ease.

'I'm on *your* side, Mrs Thompson. I am very disturbed by all I've learned. I assure you again that I am not involved in this affair, but I do want to get to the bottom of it. You will realise that my hands are very tied because I have no powers to operate and no authority to go around asking questions. That doesn't stop me from being curious and indeed disturbed about certain matters appertaining to your husband's death. I have many trustworthy and honest friends in the force and I'm sure they will help me find the truth. If you can see your way to trust me, I'll certainly try to discover what's been going on.'

My speech had put her in a quandary. Her first impassioned outburst was a genuine cry for help and now she distrusted me. In her mind, I might even be one of the killers and a police-spy, but I had to gain her trust because she might possess vital information. For one thing, she might put my mind at rest in deciding whether the Special Branch or the Security Service had eliminated Thompson. If they *had*, then there was something seriously amiss and I knew—or I thought I knew—that no loyal British official would resort to that type of tactic. If Thompson had been 'officially' eliminated, then there were traitors and criminals in high places and within both Services. In itself, that was of major concern, but how could I find out?

If there were traitors in high authority, why would they invent a plot to get rid of

MacIntyre and disguise it as an 'official' matter? I could swallow the story they'd told me at Richmond. If MacIntyre was suspected of being traitorous, then he must be removed from his position of authority. That had to be done at any cost and their method seemed a good way of achieving this. With reservations, I approved of it. The end can sometimes justify the means.

But, I told myself, if the plot was genuine and designed to fulfil that task, then murder should never enter into it. I could not believe that kind of crime would be sanctioned even for the sake of state security. It became very clear to me that, had I not stumbled into the plot, no one would have connected that murder with the MacIntyre plot. No one. Thompson would have handed over his code, been disposed of and his body dumped over Boulby cliffs. If the crash had not occurred, no one would have known of his meeting at Carlton; his job at the Cleveland Tontine would not be regarded as relevant because no member of the public or even the police would know of MacIntyre's presence there as he'd used a false name. And on top of that, two police forces were involved—Cleveland Police were investigating the murder because the body had been found in their area many miles from the Tontine, and they had no reason to connect him with the crashed plane. Then I'd given my statement. Suddenly, everything was connected.

There were so many 'ifs'—if the entire plot was false, the fact that the murdered corpse was in one police force's area and the crashed plane in another was a further insurance that the two incidents would remain totally unconnected in the minds of the investigating teams. I had provided the link, an accident had provided the link. I couldn't escape the fact that if I had not found the crash—or if the crash had not occurred—Thompson's death would have been treated as the minor murder of a small-time crook.

In truth, this was far from the case. For one thing, he was no small-time crook. He was a professional mercenary, one who was used by many organisations for their devious plans.

My thinking came to an abrupt halt as I realised that Mrs Thompson was staring at me. I'd been gazing into space as I pondered those points but returned my attention to her.

'I'm sorry,' I apologised. 'I was working out what might have happened. Forgive me.'

'Perhaps I ought to be going,' she had almost finished her lager. 'I mustn't drink any more because I'm driving.'

'I am going to look into this affair, Mrs Thompson,' I told her. 'I'm not at all happy about it and I may want more help from you.'

'From me? What sort of help?'

'I don't know yet but I'll appreciate anything you can give. Obviously, someone was in touch with your husband before he met the aircraft's pilot—or before he met me! Someone arranged it all. Who was it? Has anyone called at your house? How was contact made with your husband? Did the police ever call? If so, which officer was it?'

In spite of my earnest desire to learn the truth, I could see that she was not prepared to trust me. She said, 'I'll think very hard about it.'

'I'll be in touch with you again,' I smiled. 'Could I have your address?'

I got the impression she didn't really want to supply it, but she did; anyway, I could have found out from her car number or from the telephone directory or even through the electoral register. She did shake hands with me before she left the Moorcock.

I escorted her to her car and noted its number; as she unlocked the door I said, 'I'm sorry about the events of the past few days, Mrs Thompson. Please feel you can trust me.'

'Thank you,' was all she said. I watched the white mini roar from the car park and decided she was a nice girl, a wife any husband could be proud of but I knew she'd never trust another policeman. Never.

That self-same worry now rested upon my shoulders. If there was an underhand plot, whom could I trust? To date, I'd blandly accepted all that had been explained to me and wondered if I'd been too naïve. My thoughts went back to that office in Richmond; in the presence of the chief constable and Detective Chief Superintendent Bird, I'd been told, and had accepted, that Thompson's murder was the possible work of a thug who wanted the cash. All present had seemed to accept that explanation. Who had put it forward?

Riley! Detective Sergeant Riley of the Metropolitan Police Special Branch had adeptly twisted our concern about the murder into a suggestion that we thought *MacIntyre* had killed Thompson! Then he'd demolished our supposed worries by saying there was no reason to think that MacIntyre was concerned in the killing. And the Chief Constable, with the rest, had accepted that. We had all agreed that MacIntyre was an unlikely suspect for Riley had had him under surveillance for about a week.

But not one of us had given one iota of attention to the possibility that the *plotters* against MacIntyre might have disposed of Thompson. It was his widow's words which had jerked me to my senses. 'He would know too much to be allowed to live'. It was possible that I now knew more than Thompson!

It doesn't take a genius to realise that I was treading on very dangerous ground. If what I suspected was true—and if I took steps to prove it or even to satisfy my own curiosity—it was possible that I'd finish up with a bullet through my head. Put there by whom?

I unlocked the car and started the

engine. I was convenient for Stokesley which lay some fifteen minutes drive from here and decided to pop into the police station to see what further developments there'd been. It was the ideal starting point for my search for the truth.

During the drive, I realised that the real solution lay in Reginald George MacIntyre himself. Suppose he *wasn't* a left-wing subversive? If he was totally innocent of those allegations, why go to all this trouble to bully him into premature retirement?

I decided to examine the matter from that angle to see if I came up with a different set of answers. I drove slowly, giving rise to hoots and flashing lights from the more impatient motorists, but ignored them in their ire. I had to completely re-think the case and it wasn't easy.

MacIntyre is innocent, I told myself. Consider an illegal set-up within the police or the Security Service, a set-up designed to discredit him. He is accused of something and is framed so thoroughly that he cannot prove his innocence. Thus his character is destroyed and he is totally obliterated from public life. But why? Why do that to an innocent man?

They said he was a left-wing subversive,

but suppose he was as honest and as true as any Englishman should be? Suppose he knew something and because of his knowledge, they, the extremists, wanted rid of him? Suppose they wanted to silence him?

My head was aching with the combined effort of concentrating upon both the road and the variety of circumstances that presented themselves. And on top of that, why would an innocent man arrive at an hotel—and one only a few miles from his home—under a false name? That, if anything, implied some form of guilt and the room *was* a double room. I reflected on Mrs England's arrival—she'd wanted to surprise her 'husband' but I knew the explanation for her piece of romantic play-acting. But someone had booked that room. Someone had booked a double room, so that someone must have known MacIntyre's assumed name. Was it Thompson? Or Riley? Or someone else?

Thompson had worked there as a waiter and he was instrumental in passing the coded message bearing England's name, so *he'd* known that MacIntyre was to use that pseudonym. According to Mrs Thompson, the job had been planned by the police. That meant the police knew of his assumed name. But which police?

I began to suspect that his trip to the Tontine may have been official and one which some factions wished to prevent or interrupt. If he'd arranged to stay overnight there under his assumed name, it may well have been for very secret and important reasons. That being so, there would be a handful of persons who knew about it—only a handful—thus it became possible that someone had betrayed him and his purpose. Again, I had to ask—who?

Thompson knew his adopted name and his estimated time of arrival and had ferried that information to the plotters for £25,000. But Thompson was working *for* the police, not against them. Did this make sense?

Nothing made sense any more! I'd reached the stage where I didn't feel that I could trust anyone. If there was a deep conspiracy, anyone of any rank or position within the police service might be involved, and by talking to the wrong person I could risk my neck—and more besides—if I wasn't careful.

I reached Stokesley and found the police station in darkness, so I continued until I joined the A.19 and headed south. This meant passing the Cleveland Tontine so I decided to pop in. I'd had nothing to eat since tea-time and fancied a bar-snack.

The first person I saw in the bar was Detective Sergeant Riley.

TEN

I let him buy me a pint and by way of opening the conversation he asked what I was doing over here. I told him I'd been to Loftus where I'd identified Thompson as the man to whom I'd passed the cash. This was possibly his first intimation that I'd spoken to Cleveland Police about Thompson but his face concealed any hostile reaction to my news. He went on to ask if I had been home since then; I said I had and that I'd then gone out to visit a friend. I didn't tell him who it had been, but implied it was an illicit lady friend who'd had to go home early. I fancied a meal here, hence my visit to the Tontine.

Whether he was making polite conversation or subtly quizzing me, I wasn't

135

sure but I was sufficiently intelligent not to openly lie. I could have said I'd never been home and that I'd stayed on at Loftus to visit friends, but I was quite aware of the fact that my movements could now be under surveillance. I ordered scampi and chips and he decided to do likewise; he'd been working late and had missed the hotel dinner. It was inevitable that we talked about MacIntyre and my replies became guarded as I realised that he was quizzing me. He asked my opinion on the operation as a whole, and I pretended to accept Thompson's death as something quite divorced from the MacIntyre plot. I agreed that it was possibly the work of greedy thugs and let him do most of the talking because he seemed strangely anxious to tell me of his part in the affair.

It had been engineered by the Security Service, he said, and although they frequently sought police assistance their policy was never to ask the police to break the law. If the law had to be broken to achieve the desired result, then the Security Service, through its network of agents, would take that risk. In plots of this nature, the police, through the medium of the Special Branch, are frequently consulted and occasionally involved. In this case, they'd helped to establish the plan which had the full approval of the Home Office.

It seemed important to him that I believed the plot had been officially approved, that it wasn't his idea and that he, like me, was a mere pawn in the hands of greater mortals.

I assured him that I accepted all he told me and that I had no axe to grind. I was merely a witness, I repeated and bought the next round. When the basket meals arrived I seized the opportunity to query the identity of the pilot.

'I don't know his name,' he shook his head. 'But I can tell you it was someone hired by the Security Service. It may have been one of their own agents or it may have been a freelance pilot. They'll never admit their part in that, of course, because the plane was "borrowed"—the correct legal term is that it was taken without the owner's consent. In this plan, great secrecy was needed and the intention was to use it and then return it after the operation, replete with fuel and re-painted in its original colours. On Saturday, it was taken from a small airfield near the Sussex coast, having been ear-marked some time ago. It was known that the owner was overseas and wouldn't miss it.

'It was flown up to Buckinghamshire where it was painted overnight to remove its identification marks and used on Sunday the carry the money. Unfortunately it crashed and we know the rest. The local police will never learn the reason for its flight.'

'Why go to all that trouble?' I asked. 'Wouldn't a car or the railways have been good enough to transport the money?'

'They would, but it was a question of time. We had to act extremely quickly once we knew MacIntyre's time of arrival at the Tontine. Thompson wouldn't tell us until he had the cash in his hands.'

'Was the pilot experienced?'

Riley nodded. 'Very. The Security Service always use the best when it wants some dirty work done, Mr Metcalfe! Even the best pilots can make errors—the error this fellow made is a very common one, even among airliners. It was a blessing you found the money. A dishonest person could have ruined our plans.'

It still bothered me that this man knew

of the date, time and place of MacIntyre's arrival in spite of the fact that I'd deposited the code at Stokesley Police Station. I didn't seek clarification because I didn't trust him. I didn't trust anyone and for the time being, I didn't want him to know that I had the slightest cause to suspect that things weren't as he tried to make me believe.

We changed the subject and I said I'd have to be getting home. It was a long drive on roads which might be icy and I left him soon after ten-thirty. I was home by quarter past eleven, tired but content, and made myself a cup of hot, sweet cocoa. I sat at the kitchen table to drink and began to doodle on an old envelope which had contained a circular.

I found myself working out a suitable plot involving all those characters and with a pencil mark, I linked those I knew to be connected with one another. I began with Herriott.

Owing to the nature of their individual work, Herriott must know MacIntyre, so I drew a straight line between those men. Herriott also knew or was connected with, both Pierce and Riley. I drew another connecting line. The Tontine Inn featured strongly in the affair and I knew that MacIntyre, Riley and Pierce were all connected with that inn. Herriott, to my knowledge, was not. I therefore linked the respective parties with the inn. Thompson seemed to be in the centre of the activity so I put him in the middle of my doodle which was growing into a recognisable chart. He was also linked with the Tontine; he was connected with Riley and/or Pierce because they'd all been in the hotel at one and the same time. To my knowledge, there was no direct connection between Thompson and Herriott, nor between Thompson and MacIntyre. From what Riley had just told me, the pilot appeared to have been selected by Herriott and he could be a link between Herriott and Thompson. As things had worked out, that link was never completed. I realised there could have been a link between Thompson and MacIntyre, through his chauffeur or a maid (if he had one) or even through one of Thompson's expert burglaries. Thompson might have planted the pornographic books (if he wasn't already dead by that time). I drew a connecting line.

The other participant was the prostitute. I knew of her connection with Thompson and with the Tontine; her connection with MacIntyre had been engineered through Thompson whose connection with MacIntyre was also through the Tontine.

Pressure must have been exerted by high authority upon Herriott to compel him to fashion the plot, but for what reason? Was it simply to counter MacIntyre's secret life and have him dismissed, or could it be for more sinister reasons? I wondered if he was engaged upon some secret work which, if allowed to proceed, was dangerous to leftist elements? I wrote above his name 'Secret Mission' to see how the whole thing looked.

My chart appeared like this:

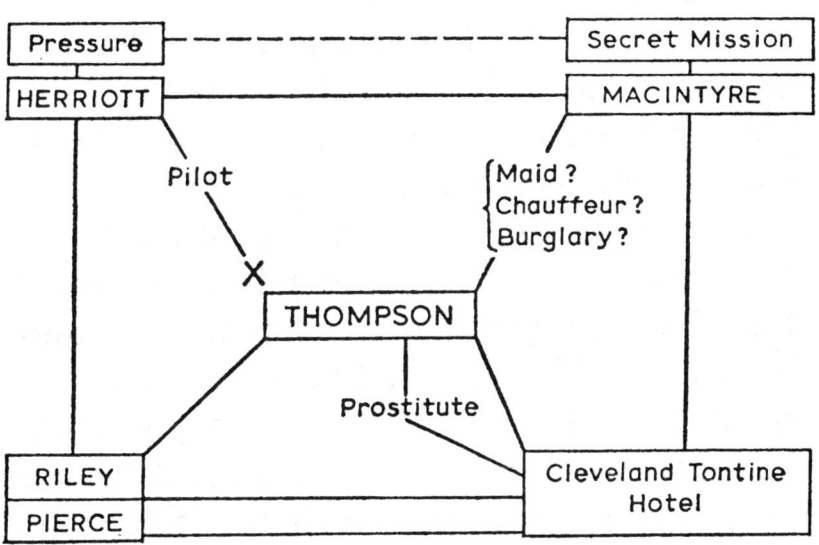

I did wonder if there had been a connection between Herriott's bosses and MacIntyre's supposed secret mission, as I termed the unknown factor, so I drew a dotted line to suggest the possibility.

Once the plot had been reduced to paper, it was simplified and I could see that because Thompson had been in the centre of activities, it *was* possible that he had known too much. Was it too much to be allowed to live?

The prostitute with the Welsh name, Alison Jean Jenkins, had no apparent connection with anyone else, for her link with MacIntyre had been achieved through Thompson. Of all the persons in the set-up, she was the one most likely to have a story to tell and that, I realised, could put her life in danger. If, due to her activities, the plot had been blown, she may have been eliminated, like Thompson.

I knew her name—and having regard to the nature of the job she'd undertaken, I found it strange that her identity should be known. Thompson had taken a lot of trouble to obtain a set of false registration plates for his car and yet the girl had arrived quite openly in a car which was traceable. And we'd traced it. Me and Gerry at York.

Had I told Riley and Pierce that I knew her? I didn't think I'd told anyone—but on reflection, I found it odd that she'd left herself so vulnerable—unless the car, like the Bulldog, had been borrowed or stolen, or had been sporting false plates.

The only way to find out was to interview the registered owner. I had friends in my late force who would do that for me, but I knew no one in her part of the country. Besides, on an enquiry of this nature, the personal interview is vital—to adequately explain the ramifications of the incident through a third party is nigh impossible and if I chose to go through semi-official channels, it would mean asking Gerry Sullivan to ring someone in the south and in turn to explain the complications to that person. The story would lose a lot in the process and apart from that, I was one of the few individuals who could say whether Alison Jean Jenkins was the Mrs England who had been at the Tontine that day.

I decided, there and then, to drive down myself. I had nothing to lose and my action should pass unnoticed by anyone. Her distance from the scene would shield my movements and the fact that she'd been recruited by Thompson meant the others had had no dealings with her. It was possible that they didn't know her by name, although both Riley and Pierce had seen her in the Tontine. I had her address—at least, I had *an* address and that was a starting point.

It wasn't too late, so I could ring her now to see if she would be available tomorrow. I picked up the phone and dialled Directory Enquiries. Upon my call being accepted, I heard a distant click on my line; it was similar to the click that occurs when a person is listening in on a party line. I knew my phone was no longer private.

So I *was* being supervised! I thought rapidly; if I slammed down the receiver, they'd realise that I had tumbled to their ruse, so I asked Enquiries for a number I didn't want. I told the girl I wanted the phone number of *The Farmers Weekly*, a London based agricultural magazine and when this was provided I replaced the phone, thanking her and saying I'd ring the editor in the morning.

The fact that my involvement had created an unhealthy interest in someone's mind meant that there was no time to lose. I'd drive south immediately; I'd strike while the iron was hot, as they say. I had sufficient ready cash to buy petrol en route and within quarter of an hour I'd locked the house and was easing the car from the garage.

My intention was to head for Thirsk and thence to the Great North Road from which I would eventually enter the M.1. But as I drove out of the village, a set of headlights came up behind me. A car eased out of the unmade road which led to the parish church, and began to follow. For the first four or five miles along our narrow country lanes, this was nothing out of the ordinary. These lanes made it difficult for anyone to overtake and processions of vehicles were a regular feature in the North Yorkshire moors and dales.

Upon reaching Coxwold, I would normally have turned right, but the click on my telephone made me realise I was a likely victim of a shadowing operation. I decided to change my route. I'd test him. I would meander through the byways, going via Husthwaite and across country to Boroughbridge, there to join the A.1.

He came with me. I tested him once or twice by taking little known diversions, or by driving slowly then accelerating apparently without reason. He emulated every act and movement and I knew my car wasn't fast enough to shake him off. He made no secret that he was shadowing me and by constantly glancing in my mirror, I saw he was alone.

Content in that knowledge, I settled down to a steady drive. I hoped to catch sight of his face through my mirror or perhaps a glimpse of his registration plate, but the brilliance of his lights and the distance he maintained to my rear prevented that. I led him to the south-bound carriageway of the Great North Road at Boroughbridge. It was now twelve-thirty in the morning. Saturday.

After driving down the M.1. for some way, I pulled into Woodall Service Station to take a rest and to buy some petrol. I was followed in by several vehicles and at this stage wasn't sure whether my tail was still with me. In the darkness, one pair of headlights is like most others and any one of them could have been my shadow. By the time I'd parked and locked my car, they had distributed themselves all over the parking area and I saw no one that I recognised. That, in itself, meant little but I took a stroll around the parking lot to stretch my legs and took deep breaths of cool night air. During my perambulations, I recognised no one, nor could I identify a vehicle. I had a coffee and a sandwich, then continued south. Three cars followed me out; another one had been parked on the hard-shoulder just south of the Service Station and he followed me too. That was him—he'd never come in ...

During the entire trip my mirror was full of headlights and my shadow could stay behind without hindrance. I couldn't hope to throw him off, or anyone who may have taken over from him, before reaching the Metropolis. Once among the city traffic, I would take evasive action and began to formulate my plans. I hit London before six-thirty, having had another stop, and prepared to enter the city. The darkness was lifting and I was among the thickening city traffic, not knowing whether my tail had remained with me. I could take no chances.

My first dodge was to drive into one of those car parks where the barrier automatically lifts as you enter. It did that and even at this hour, the place was filling rapidly. Several cars followed me in. I circled for a while and parked in one of the spaces provided. There I sat for a few minutes, in the car, giving myself the appearance of being busy. I checked the dashboard, looked at maps, emptied ash-trays. In fact I was seeking parking tickets, bus tickets, cinema tickets or something similar. Having found some of each, I placed them all together in a little thick wad and took a 10p piece from my pocket. This would let me out of the car park. I compared my wad of paper with it; it was about the same width, although a shade more square! I tore it to roughly the size of the coin.

Having done this, I drove towards the exit; I pressed in the coin and followed immediately with the wad of paper, pushing it tightly home. This effectively prevented anyone else from inserting a coin and I pushed it in far enough to prevent anyone easily digging it out with their fingers or a knife. You'd have to dismantle the machine to free it.

Once through the barrier, I slowed down to see if anyone tried to leave behind me. A grey Vauxhall began to ease out and I was sure the driver was my old friend Tweedledum—Detective Constable Pierce! I accelerated into the traffic before

I could be completely certain and I think I lost him. I didn't see him get through the barrier. I parked in a multi-storey car-park near Holloway and took a tube from there. My next task was to see if the London Underground trains would take me anywhere near Shamblebury.

ELEVEN

Thanks to a combination of tube trains, buses and a taxi, I found myself in Shamblebury before nine o'clock. Feeling distinctly unwashed, unshaved and scruffy, I located a gents' loo where I did the necessary and emerged with a freshly shining face, combed hair and a desire for eggs, bacon and toast thick with marmalade, and all washed down with hot, sweet coffee.

I discovered a small café which performed the miracle of breakfast and twenty minutes later set off, on foot, to locate Carthew House. It was a mansion-style house with ivy on the walls and enhanced by massive portals with pseudo-Roman pillars. Stone lions lay at rest on each side of the steps and a neat perpendicular row of door bells told me it had been converted into a block of flats. I found Miss Jenkins' name opposite the ground floor bell. So far, so good.

I repeatedly rang it and waited; I thought she must be out and was about to leave when a woman in a housecoat appeared in the gloomy inner sanctum. I recognised her as Mrs England. So her car number *had* been genuine! She opened the door looking tired and pale, but nonetheless sexy even if she had been roused from her beauty sleep.

'Yes?' her voice was cultured and she blinked against the bright light of day.

'Miss Jenkins?' I asked.

She nodded and hugged the coat tightly around her slender body.

'I'd like to speak to you on a rather urgent and private matter,' I emphasised the latter words. 'Is it convenient?'

'Are you from the police?' her face was devoid of expression.

I shook my head. 'No. My name is Metcalfe—Martin Metcalfe. I'm a friend of Mrs Thompson, the wife of Paul Thompson.'

'Paul Thompson?' it was difficult to judge if her questioning of his name was genuine or contrived; her face continued to reveal nothing of her thoughts.

'You did a little job for him in Yorkshire,' I watched her eyes. 'At the Cleveland Tontine Hotel.'

'Go on,' she spoke with absolutely no change of expression nor admission of that role.

'I'd like to talk to you about it.'

'I didn't say I knew him nor did I say I had been involved in any job in Yorkshire.'

'But you were, Miss Jenkins. I saw you arrive—you followed me into the hotel and you booked in under the name of Mrs England.'

'Are you her solicitor? Or a private detective? There was nothing like that in it.'

'I'm a friend of Mrs Thompson, no more. I'm out of work, if you wish to know that. I'm not a private detective, nor a policeman, nor a solicitor. I'm nothing—just a friend of Mrs Thompson.'

'What do you want?'

She seemed loath to let me enter the house and preferred to stand on the

151

doorstep in the cold wind.

'He's dead,' I said bluntly. 'He was shot in the head and his body was dumped over the cliffs between Whitby and Saltburn.'

'Oh God!' this time there was a reaction. 'You'd better come in, Mr Metcalfe.'

She led me into her kitchen. It was a spacious affair with white furnishings, including an automatic washing machine, dish washer, and other Colour Supplement essentials. She indicated a chair at the table and asked if I'd like a coffee. I said, 'Yes,' even though I'd just had one. She busied herself at the gas cooker with a pan of milk, alone with her thoughts and hiding her face from me. I looked for indications of tears, but there were none.

'His wife wants me to find out what he was involved in,' I said quietly.

'Do they know who killed him?' she spoke with her back to me, watching the milk rise in the pan.

'No,' I said. 'No one's been traced, so far as I am aware.'

'You said you saw me at the Cleveland Tontine, Mr Metcalfe,' she turned towards me, very assured and bearing two cups of steaming coffee, each with thick milky foam on top. 'Why were you there?'

152

I told her without revealing all my knowledge of the plot against MacIntyre, but I did make her aware that I knew of the work she'd undertaken from time to time for Thompson.

'It's that aspect of this business that Mrs Thompson wants me to find out. She wants to know what you and her husband were engaged upon.'

'Why?'

'She thinks the police killed him,' I said, slowly sipping from the hot rim of the cup. 'I promised to find out as much as I could—it's for her peace of mind, more than anything. She daren't tell the police of her suspicions in case they harm her or cover up the incident. She asked me to help,' and I told Miss Jenkins how Mrs Thompson had come to ask me.

'Do the police know about me?' she asked.

I had to think hard. Riley and Pierce had seen her in the hotel, but did they know her identity? I'd found her through her registration number but had I mentioned it in any of my statements? I thought not. I'd mentioned it to my pal, Gerry Sullivan in York, but couldn't recall telling Riley and Pierce, or anyone else, about the M.G.B.

car. It was possible, of course, that Riley and Pierce knew through Thompson.

'I don't know,' I had to admit.

'So how did you know of me?' was her next question. 'Thompson wouldn't tell you.'

'I traced you through your car number. I've friends in the Taxation Departments who checked it for me.' This was a white lie—I didn't want her to know I had friends in the police. 'I saw it at the Tontine—a nice blue M.G.B. I find it odd that you used a car so readily traceable on a mission which was supposed to be very secret.'

'I was told to, at the last minute. Thompson wanted me to use it.'

'Did he say why?'

'I don't know you, do I? How do I know I can trust you?'

'You don't, I'm afraid. And I don't know if I can trust you. It's a decision only you can make.'

She stared at me, her eyes now clear and beautiful, and the colour returning to her cheeks. She had a lovely and expressive face and began to talk. Initially, Thompson had insisted on absolute secrecy on that mission but for no apparent reason he'd changed his mind before finalising the plans. He'd told her to use an identifiable car and to be prepared to give evidence before any court of law or at any enquiry in respect of her actions connected with MacIntyre. She did not know why he'd said that, but he had insisted on those conditions before accepting her for the role. She would be highly paid, he'd assured her. She told me that Thompson had travelled south to see her about it and to outline his requirements. Later, when the plans had been finalised, she was to report at the Cleveland Tontine as near as possible to 5 p.m. on that Thursday. She was to give the name 'Mrs England' and to say her husband would be late. She had to obtain the bedroom key and get there first to surprise him. 'England' had originally booked a single room but the booking had been changed to a double one, without MacIntyre's knowledge. Thompson, acting as a waiter, had engineered that.

Upon England's arrival, she was to use a pistol to detain him in his room, behind a locked door, until the police came. If he got there first, she was to knock on his door and enter at his response, using the pistol to keep him inside. When the police came to his door, but before allowing them into the room, she had to hide the gun. There would be time to conceal it under the mattress. She could leave when the police raid was over, although her name may be taken. It was expected the raid would occur the same night as her arrival. Those were her terms of reference. The police who called would also have their terms of reference. I knew that, because Riley and Pierce had executed that raid. They would 'find' the hidden gun, but I could almost guarantee that no further mention of it would be made, and should MacIntyre allege he'd been held at gunpoint, they'd deny all knowledge of a weapon. MacIntyre would appear to be a liar.

When I asked about the gun, she said she had been told that it would be handed to her during her journey north. This would be done in Thirsk by a man in the Rose Café at 4 p.m. on that Thursday. He would recognise her—at the same time, she'd get an advance of part of her fee. She'd acted in accordance with her instructions and had entered the café at 4 p.m. where a man had handed a brief-case to her. It had contained a small automatic pistol, with ammunition, and half her fee, i.e. £2,500. She was promised the remaining £2,500 upon completion of the operation, if successful. Thompson would pay it, the man assured her.

So far she hadn't received the balance but had not raised a fuss because Thompson was always fair, straight and business-like in his dealings with her. She trusted him; they'd worked together many times.

News of his death had shocked her, but she'd borne it well. When I questioned her about the brief-case received in Thirsk, it appeared to be identical with the others, a black solid executive type with the initials 'P.B.G.' on the lid.

'Where is it now?' I asked.

'In my bedroom. I took the gun out and put the case in the boot of my car, with the cash. I hoped no one would steal the car from the Tontine but they didn't. I had nowhere else to keep it, had I? It's in the bank now. I put the gun in my handbag and took it into the hotel.'

'Tell me about the actual raid—when England's room was searched.'

'I'd managed to keep him in the room as I'd been instructed, and had locked the bedroom door. I kept the key. He gave me no trouble at all, but kept asking what it was all about. I couldn't tell him because I didn't know ...'

'Did you know? I mean, had you been told what was really going on?'

'No, I was just obeying orders.'

'Did you know who your Mr England was?'

'No,' she said with all sincerity and I believed her. 'I had no idea. You mentioned a Mr MacIntyre, so I guess "England" was a false name.'

'It was,' I said. 'But go on.'

'I'd kept him there, chatting and so on until about eleven-thirty that night. He'd unpacked and was in a chair, reading a paperback. He seemed to be totally unflustered and refused to go to bed.'

'Did you suggest joining him? In bed, I mean?'

'No, it wasn't that kind of assignment. Then just after eleven-thirty, there was a knock on the door and I asked who it was.'

'You asked? Not him?'

'I asked. He just sat and said nothing. I was expecting the police, you see. A voice said, "Police. Open the door." I hid the gun under the mattress as I'd been told and then opened the door. They came in and took Mr England away. He didn't protest and they didn't ask me any questions, other than my name and address.'

'Did you give your real name and address?'

'Yes, Thompson said I must.'

'That means the police *do* know your identity!' I said. 'Did they say why they'd come?'

'No. They flashed an identity card of some sort and said they were Special Branch. They took him away. It was all over in a few seconds.'

'Did they search the room?'

'Not at that time. They may have returned. I left the gun where I'd hidden it.'

'Did you stay?'

'No, I left too. I saw the receptionist and said I'd had an urgent call to return home. I paid the bill,' and she laughed. 'Bed and breakfast for two. Then I drove straight home.'

'Without the rest of your fee?'

'Yes, I trusted Thompson. I've told you that.'

'Think back to the policemen who raided

that bedroom. Did you know them? Had you seen them before?'

She shook her head.

'Can you describe them?'

There was little doubt she described Riley and Pierce. She repeated she'd never seen them before and when I pointed out that they had been resident in the hotel, she said she'd gone straight to the bedroom. She'd not set foot in any other part of the premises, and her account agreed with what I had seen. When I asked her to describe the fellow who had handed her the brief-case in Thirsk, she wasn't very helpful.

I had thought it may have been Riley or Pierce, but she didn't think so. It wasn't Thompson either, so it could have been someone working for him.

'Can I see the brief-case please?'

'Do you know what's happening, Mr Metcalfe? Paul didn't tell me and I didn't ask. We reckoned that the less we knew, the less there was to give away.'

I told her a little. I revealed the identity of England and that alone shocked her. If she'd known who he was, she'd have thought twice about entering a plot to frame an H.M.I. I said it was intended to bring about his resignation for reasons not quite clear to me. I told her that the Security Service were behind the plot, aided by the police.

'But *they* wouldn't kill Paul, would they?'

'No,' I shook my head. 'But that's exactly what Mrs Thompson thinks has happened. She thought he knew too much to be allowed to remain alive—she knew the police had commissioned him for the job ...'

'Good God! I see what you're getting at. Are you trying to say it was a false plot, Mr Metcalfe?' She was no fool.

'I'm just trying to find out, Miss Jenkins. I was hoping you might be able to assist.'

'I'm sorry. I haven't been very helpful, have I? I'll fetch that brief-case for you.'

She left the kitchen and I heard her slippers padding along the passage to another room. I was contemplating the possibility that I'd revealed too much when the door bell rang and I heard her hurry from her bedroom. She handed the case in to me as she passed the kitchen door and as he rang again, she called, 'All right, all right. I'm coming.'

I left the chair and carried the case to

the window for a better look and was surprised to hear her give a sharp cry of fear as a man's voice said, 'Not a whisper, lady. Now get inside.'

I knew that bloody voice! I moved across the kitchen to be near the open door, hoping to catch their words and slid into a vacant space behind it. I was hidden by the door as I stood between it and the washing machine. Was it one of her customers? A pimp? A strong arm man wanting his share of her earnings?

They were coming this way. I was about to leap back into the centre of the kitchen to pretend I hadn't been listening when I heard her call, 'Put that gun away ...'

'Shut up!' was his reply.

I remained where I was, completely hidden from him even if he entered the kitchen. I clutched the heavy brief-case in my right hand. She led him into the kitchen but didn't turn to find out where I'd gone. I knew she was relying on me; testing me perhaps? The man followed, pressing a snub-nosed Walther into her back.

I recognised that broad back. I knew those heavy shoulders and those big loose jowls Tweedledum! Detective Constable

Pierce in person. He was fully into the kitchen and standing about eighteen inches in front of me, totally unaware of my presence.

'You worked for Thompson?' he growled at her.

'Why do you ask?'

'Out with it, woman. What did he tell you about the MacIntyre job?'

'Nothing.'

'You're lying, you bitch!' and he raised his fat hand to deliver a blow to her head. She couldn't see his action, but the movement made the pistol waver from the small of her back. His intended blow never landed because I raised the brief-case above my head, holding it with both hands, and brought it down with all my might upon the nape of his thick neck.

TWELVE

The force of my blow sent the case spinning from my hands as he staggered forward, off balance. I kicked him to accelerate his downfall and sailed in to finish him. My surprise attack, aided by the kick on his ample backside, was sufficient to knock him to the floor but he was far from unconscious, nor was he disabled. The woman had backed off and stood in a corner with her hands at her mouth as I leapt forward to stamp upon his gun hand. He moved just as quickly and I missed; he scrambled on all fours to dodge my onslaught and as I recovered from that forward leap, he used the Welsh dresser to drag himself to his feet.

I took the opportunity to leap on to his wide back and managed to lock my right forearm beneath his chin. My left hand gripped that wrist and I exerted all my strength to haul back his massive head. I could feel my bony arm pressing into his soft throat and he began to succumb to that pressure. His breathing became harsh and strained as he tried to say something. His arms were flailing about, weakly.

'The gun!' I shouted at the woman. 'Take it off him!'

She hovered uncertainly; I clung to his huge and powerful back like a limpet. He tried to dislodge me and we crashed about the kitchen. Over went her table and with it several pieces of crockery which shattered across the floor and then I managed to fell him by hooking one of my legs between his as we milled around. Off balance, he crashed to the floor among the broken plates, somehow not cutting himself, and my fall was cushioned by his bulk. His gun arm descended with his weight behind it and it crunched across an overturned chair. The pain must have been awful because he howled as the Walther was sent spinning from his hand, carving a path through the debris to disappear beneath the cooker.

'Get it!' I screamed and she got to her knees to retrieve it. We had him now; my forearm continued to press into his soft throat and suddenly I released him. Before he could move away, I delivered a rabbit punch to his neck. His head slumped forward; I'd hit the right place and he fell to the floor. He'd be unconscious for a few minutes, that's all. Alison Jenkins had recovered the Walther and brushed the dust from it before handing it over. She smiled her gratitude.

As Pierce lay groaning at my feet, I searched him. I removed his wallet and took out the warrant card, then located his car keys in another pocket. I examined all his possessions and returned everything except the warrant card and the keys. I was no thief. Apart from the Walther automatic, he had nothing else of interest, but I now had his gun and his warrant card.

'You'll have to leave here,' I was saying to her as I concluded my search. 'He may not be alone and more of his pals might come to deal with you. Have you anywhere to go?'

'I've a flat in town. I use it—for work,' and she smiled, rather coyly, I thought.

'Could they find it?'

'I think the police have a record of all prostitutes' addresses.'

'You'd better get dressed and fetch some things with you. We'll go to that address for the time being. We should be all right there for an hour or two because Pierce won't be able to get a message to his cronies. I'll see to that. There are one or two things I must do before we leave here. Did this chap come by car?'

'Yes, it's parked in my drive.'

'I'll take his car into town and will

follow you. We'll tie him up and stick him in the rear seat of his own car, then I'll dump him, and the car, in a car-park somewhere.'

She hurried away to dress and to pack. Meanwhile, Pierce recovered. He sat up and blinked owlishly at me as he began to rub his bruised neck. I was seated above him with his Walther in my hands. It was loaded, I'd checked; and it was now pointing unerringly at his head.

'Oh, it's you,' was all he said as he tried to get to his feet. 'Where the hell did you spring from?'

'Sit still,' I ordered and my eyes never left his big frame for one second.

'What's going on, Metcalfe? Why are you here and what the hell did you do that for?' he was twisting and turning his head to ease the pain.

'To stop you from hurting the lady.' I didn't smile.

'Look, you bloody fool, I'm on official police business—you realise that this prostitute is mixed up with MacIntyre?'

'I do. And I also know that no police officer is authorised to use a firearm on a routine enquiry and even if you fellows *are* issued with guns, the Walther is not

167

on official issue, is it?'

He stared at me, his watery eyes blinking.

'You're in this far too bloody deeply, Mr Metcalfe.'

'Not me, Mr Pierce. You're the one who's in too deep. By the accident of my involvement your plans have misfired and their link with Thompson's death has put some unstoppable wheels in motion. I know a good deal more than you believe and I'm one jump ahead of you. To Thompson's cost, he wasn't.'

The beaten man said nothing in return but I knew I'd scored a hit. Even so, I had no real idea of their missions or plans. I had to rely on bluff, never easy against a professional.

'You'll never prove anything against us,' he ventured. 'It's too late. Thompson poked his nose into too many corners and look what's happened to him.'

'On the contrary,' I countered, 'it's never too late. There's a traitor among your lot, Mr Pierce. Grow up! We know what's been going on ...'

'You bastards!' and from that moment he said nothing else. I tried to coax and goad him into talking but the strong and silent Pierce shut up like the proverbial clam.

'It's an old and well tried police tactic to pretend, during interviews, that you know more than you really do. In that way, one can often encourage a person to talk but these tactics cut no ice with Pierce. He simply kept his mouth shut and I held him at gun point until Alison returned, this time looking like a dream.

'I'll need two pieces of rope,' I told her. 'Clothes line would be ideal. And I want a gag.'

'What are you going to do?' he stared at me with frightened eyes.

'I'm not going to drop you in the Thames!' I laughed. 'We're just going to lose you for an hour or two, that's all.'

Pierce glared at me and I knew I'd planted valuable seeds of concern in his mind. He'd be going over the plot as he knew it, looking for flaws in its arrangement and execution, or building suspicions about his colleagues. I hoped that my intervention would be construed as a planned exercise and he would surely find his traitor, even if there wasn't one!

Alison Jenkins had found a length of orange coloured plastic rope and I asked if it was in order to cut off a couple of lengths. She gave consent and so that I could fashion a gag, she'd found a headsquare and a yellow duster. In return, I asked her to take his car keys and bring his car as close as possible to the building, and park it out of sight, if possible near the back door. She said there was a space near the back door and left to carry out that small chore. When the grey Vauxhall was at the rear of this lovely old house, I jerked the Walther at him.

'Time to go,' I said and felt confident as he rose to his feet although for one horrible moment, I thought he was going to have a go at me in spite of the gun! But he didn't, he turned and led from the room. I picked up the brief-case and Alison Jenkins showed us out.

'Can you open the rear door?' I asked her when we arrived at the Vauxhall. She did so and stood back. I addressed Pierce.

'Stand near the door and face the car. Put your hands behind your back.'

Reluctantly he obeyed. I watched for any indication of open hostility but he offered none. I knew he was uncertain as to my capabilities! The girl came to my side and

I handed her the gun and followed with the brief-case.

'Point it at him and if he tries anything stupid, pull the trigger. Aim at his legs. You can't miss at this range.'

She gripped the gun confidently as her expressive eyes showed interest in my work and she never questioned my motives or my actions. She remained at my side, watching as I lashed his hands together at the wrists. I made sure the binding was very tight and my efforts drew small grunts of pain from him. Next I bound his ankles, always wary of a sudden kick but again he was docile as I hauled on the rope and knotted it to prohibit even his smallest movement.

The gag came next; after folding the yellow duster into a tight roll, I stuffed it in his mouth and secured it in position by tying the headsquare about his face. Thus trussed, I bodily turned him around so that his backside was into the car, then pushed him on the chest. He flopped onto the seat and I lifted his legs inside.

'Lie down,' I ordered as I retrieved the gun and when he obeyed, I closed the door.

'Where's your car?' I asked my hostess.

'In the garage. I'll fetch it round.'

'Are you ready to leave?'

'I've just got to collect my cases and lock the doors.'

'Fine. Bring that brief-case too, will you?' I wanted to retain it for the time being for it may be useful evidence against them. I asked her to lead me to a car-park, a multi-storey type would be ideal. I expressed a preference for one out of town and soon we were rolling down the drive, with her blue M.G.B. leading the little procession.

I adjusted my mirror so that I could keep an eye on my prostrate passenger and once or twice, he tried to heave himself into a sitting position. The first time he almost succeeded and I began to grow uneasy, wondering what he might do if he did sit up so after one or two futile attempts I waved the Walther and told him to lie still. At that, he settled down.

The M.G.B. led me to the entrance of a multi-storey car park and waited as I drove past the timing machine to disappear aloft. I found a space on the second floor and drove in. After parking the car, I locked all the doors but opened two of the windows an inch or so to provide fresh air.

'I'll ring the attendant in a few hours time, just in case no one finds you,' I assured him. 'I've got your warrant card too, so you'll have a job to prove you're a copper, won't you? I'm taking the keys with me.'

I slammed the driver's door, locked it and walked away, half expecting him to attempt to call after me or to try and kick the interior panels. But I heard no sounds, not even a muffled groan or plea for clemency. At the ground floor, I left the keys with the attendant, saying that a Mrs Bradshaw would collect them. She was my wife, I pointed out, but the truth was that by doing this I could arrange by phone to have Pierce released when I wanted. I made a note of the establishment's phone number.

'Well,' Alison Jenkins smiled as I climbed into her car. 'That was all very exciting. What was it all about?'

'I want time to find out what's going on,' I told her. 'He's a policeman but no policeman uses guns on any sort of genuine routine enquiry. Now I've got to find out what he's up to.'

'You mean you don't know?' she cried.

'Not really.'

'Good God! But it might have been a genuine enquiry! After all, he *is* a policeman.'

'Genuine? Not the way he barged into your home carrying a gun, Miss Jenkins. No policeman does that—at least, not in my part of the world!'

She laughed and said, 'Call me Alison.'

'O.K. I'm Martin,' and I offered my hand. She shook it with good humour. 'Now where do we go?'

'I'll drive you to my flat,' she offered.

On the way I told her of Pierce's role in the affair so far as I knew it and used that as my excuse for immobilising him. She thanked me and realised she may have been in danger, although neither of us knew what he'd really had in store for her. We could only guess that it was connected with her work for Thompson; Thompson had known too much. Did they think he'd imparted some of his knowledge to this woman?

Her town flat was near Portobello Road and she drew up outside a fish and chip shop to park. The smell made me realise how hungry I was, but I steeled myself against rushing in for a portion and she escorted me upstairs. Everything in her flat was of the best quality; there was genuine antique furniture, an Indian rug, thick velvet curtains with an air of opulence and privacy. There were two bedrooms; her own small private one which was cosy and moderately simple, and the 'work' room which was sumptuously furnished. The overall decor of that room was pink and feminine in the extreme for it had silken bed covers, deep-pile rugs, the best Crown wallpaper and a pervading aroma of expensive perfume.

'You're disgusted with me, aren't you?'

'No,' I answered truthfully. 'Your life is your affair, Alison. I'm no moraliser. I take you as I find you.'

'I like you,' she said. 'You're so open and frank and full of surprises.'

'But you're still suspicious of me?'

'Not any more. You must trust very strongly in your own opinions to do what you did to that big man.'

'I could be wrong, but it's too late now.'

'What do you think is happening to Mr England?'

'MacIntyre,' I corrected her. 'There is certainly a conspiracy to discredit him and if the reasons behind it are the ones given by Riley and Pierce, then I agree with them and their methods. But I don't believe they were telling the truth, yet I have no really sound evidence against them. The murder of your friend is the fly in this ointment. If they are on the wrong side of the law, that killing is their big mistake—and as if to confirm my belief, they now come after you. You're a witness, like Paul Thompson, and they carry a gun to interview you! I'm sure there's something bloody awful behind this lot, Alison.'

'You may have saved my life?' she said quietly.

'Maybe,' I agreed. 'Pierce could have taken you away to kill you. I don't think he would have done it at your home. But if that *was* his intention, then his fellow plotters are very frightened men. They'll stop at nothing now.'

'We'll be safe here for a while, won't we? If we've scared them off, they might not get access to my address, might they? Few people know it otherwise so let's have some lunch, Martin. It's gone eleven-thirty-five. You'll join me?'

'Thanks. I'd love to. What time will you be eating?'

'Twelve-thirty or thereabouts.'

'Fine. I'd like to do some rapid thinking. Do you mind if I take a walk? My brain works better when I'm walking!'

'O.K. I'll see you about twelve-thirty.'

'Lovely. Don't admit anyone you don't know. And keep the doors locked.'

She dropped the latch as I left. I took a long walk along Elgin Crescent up to Holland Park tube station and along the main road. In my mind I was turning over and re-enacting past events, although I did wonder if I was being too melodramatic. I thought of poor old Pierce imprisoned in his car and realised he could free one of the rear doors by kicking open the catch and depressing the handle with his feet. I was sure this was possible ...

But it was no good just trudging around and my mind seemed to be spinning in helpless circles. I needed urgent and professional guidance but within London's police there was no one I knew sufficiently well to trust or even to approach. I knew names; names that had appeared in the daily news and names that I had overheard from time to time in the course of my police duty, but in a situation like this you need personal contacts. Alone, I was practically helpless.

Sergeant Mortimer was one of the names I'd come across during this enquiry. He knew Pierce and Riley—he'd called them Tweedledum and Tweedledee. Could he have warned them that I was making enquiries? I remembered giving my name to him as I'd described Tweedledum and Tweedledee over Gerry Sullivan's phone. Then there was Gerry's pal, also in the Metro Special Branch. Gerry had tried to contact him that night, the night we'd made do with Mortimer. What the hell was the fellow's name?

I walked for maybe another half hour before his name came back to me. I knew it was similar to a firm of wholesalers in York, wholesale stationers. I recalled my realisation of that fact at the time. Magson was the name of the stationers—they have premises in Leeman Road at York. But that wasn't the inspector's name. I ran through the wording of Gerry's conversation once again, mentally listening to every word. Magson ... Megson! That's it. Megson. He'd asked to speak to Detective Inspector Megson.

I could trust Gerry. Of that I was

positive, but could I trust a pal of his? A pal who worked in the same department as the men I distrusted? A person I'd never met?

I had to trust someone. Although the fellow was only a name, he did provide a contact and as I pondered his trustworthiness, I thought of Alison. We scarcely knew each other and yet I'd placed an almost total trust in her and she appeared to reciprocate.

I had to make a decision. I halted in my tracks and decided to ring him. With a smart about-turn, I hurried to the kiosks near the tube station and rang the Yard. I asked for Megson by name. I was put through to the Special Branch department and repeated the name.

'Who is calling?' a girl asked.

'My name is Bradshaw,' I said, deciding not to use my own name in case it was already known there. 'It's very urgent and very personal.'

'Hold the line, sir.'

The line clicked as I was temporarily 'held' by the operator and then a deep, pleasing voice said, 'Megson speaking.'

'Gerry Sullivan from York gave me your name,' I had to establish an immediate rapport. 'I'd like to talk to you, urgently.'

'But not over the phone?'

'No,' I was adamant on that point. 'Can we meet somewhere?'

'Of course. Now?'

'Please.'

'O.K. Tell me where.'

I recalled the fish and chip shop outside Alison's flat and suggested that.

'I'll be there in about forty minutes,' he told me. 'I'm six feet two inches tall and I'll be wearing a black fur hat and a short, dark grey car coat. I've long hair, it's nearly black and I've a Mexican style moustache. I'll have a copy of *Playboy* under my left arm and will buy chips inside, but will eat them outside.'

'I'll look out for you.'

I hurried back to tell Alison and asked if I could watch the chip shop from her bedroom, the private one. She agreed and I ate my mixed grill, peaches and cream followed by coffee, from the top of her dressing table. She brought hers in too; she'd not come across Megson but five minutes after the estimated time of his arrival, I spotted him. He was eating fish and chips outside the café and the description fitted perfectly.

'Do you want to bring him here?' she invited.

'No, at least, not until I've decided whether or not I trust him. I'll leave the brief-case here for the time being.'

'You're welcome to talk here if you wish.'

'Thanks. I'm sorry about leaving the washing up! And thanks for the meal. It was great. See you soon.'

She let me out and said, 'Good luck.'

THIRTEEN

I had no idea whether or not he was alone. He appeared to be unaccompanied but it was impossible to say whether he'd brought a colleague to oversee events. I crossed the road as I left Alison's flat; he was looking away from me at the time and as I approached he turned in my direction. He was taller than I and a good deal slimmer with sunken cheeks, a dark face and very dark eyes. He looked every inch a Mexican!

All the factors he'd described were

present and I bore down upon him. He saw me and realised who I was, smiling a welcome.

'Have a chip?' was his opening gambit. I took one.

'Cheers,' I popped it into my mouth.

'Are you buying some?' he asked.

'No, I've had lunch.'

He began to walk away from the premises and I fell into step at his side.

'How is Gerry?' he asked, 'it's some time since I saw him.'

'Fine, but growing a paunch. He likes his ale too much to keep slim.'

'And the women? Is he still chasing them? He had a penchant for redheads when he was down here.'

'He married one!' I laughed. 'You should see his kids! They're like a clutch of freckled carrots!'

He laughed in return and came swiftly to our business. 'So, Mr Bradshaw, what's the panic?'

He came to rest at a bus stop; we were alone.

'Metcalfe is my real name. Martin Metcalfe. I didn't want your telephone operator to know who was calling.'

'We are cautious, aren't we? What's the trouble?'

'Does the name MacIntyre mean anything to you?' I put to him.

'Nope. Obviously you think it should.'

'He's an H.M.I. and the ex-chief constable of my old force.'

'You're in the job then?'

'Not now,' and I told him why.

'I'm sorry to hear it. But what about MacIntyre?'

I followed with a brief resume of all that had happened since Sunday. I had to break my story when a bus came and we jumped aboard where I continued my account. He'd finished his chips by this time and stuffed the paper in the bus's waste bin. I gave due import to Thompson's murder and concluded by telling him of Detective Constable Pierce's dilemma. I produced his warrant card as proof and handed it to this tall, gaunt fellow. He laughed and I kept the Walther.

'Poor old Tweedledum! Do you think he'll get free?'

'I don't know. He might attract someone's attention.'

We alighted at the next convenient stop and he took me into a pub. I bought a couple of watery pints, stuff which seemed like weak shandy when compared with the powerful Yorkshire brews to which I was accustomed. It wasn't particularly pleasant, especially after a meal but I sipped it as he produced a hooked pipe and began to prime it. It had a massive bowl and seemed to accommodate most of his tin of tobacco. Soon we were swathed in an attractively scented cloud and he said nothing as he continued to stoke up, finally producing a red and crackling glow.

'The buggers are up to something,' he said.

'I know that!' I cried. 'But what?'

'I don't know. Let's start at the beginning—that means MacIntyre. What's his Christian name?'

'Reginald George.'

'Thanks. I'll do a quick check,' and from his inside pocket he produced a slim radio set. It was a streamlined version of the type currently in use by the uniformed English policemen and was about the size of a cigarette case. Unlike a beatman's set, the transmitter and receiver were contained in one unit. He pressed a button and I saw the slender aerial spring out. We were alone in our corner as he spoke into the set.

'Megson here, Alex. Do a P.47 on the following, will you? Reginald George MacIntyre, ex-chief constable and currently an H.M.I.'

I didn't hear the reply but he sat with the set in his hand as we continued our drink. 'It'll take about ten minutes,' he told me.

He questioned me further about the events and I found myself including many details and opinions, giving due emphasis to Thompson's death and his wife's concern about it. Then the tiny radio buzzed softly.

'Megson,' he spoke quietly into it.

'He's clear,' was all I heard and Megson thanked the caller.

'The buggers are definitely up to something,' he stroked his dark moustache. 'MacIntyre's clean.'

'Clean?'

'He's not a security risk and never has been. A P.47 enquiry automatically includes a check with the Security Service. They say he's clean too. It looks as though the bastards have got into our ranks now—and there's that bloody man

Herriott too! God! If they've infiltrated the police and the Security Service, it could be terrible! We've got to do something, haven't we, Mr Metcalfe? And bloody quick too.'

'Yes,' I said, not knowing what. 'But why pick on old MacIntyre? Why plague him with a trumped up charge?'

'If we knew that we'd be half-way to discovering the motive. I must have Riley and Pierce fully investigated. And Herriott too. This means bringing in the big brass.'

'Can I add another name?'

'Sure.'

'Mortimer. He's in your department.'

'Yes, and a good chap. Why him?'

I explained how Gerry Sullivan had contacted him from York and how someone must have informed Riley and Pierce of my undue interest in their presence in Yorkshire. My own name was known to Mortimer—I'd given it myself.

'Thanks. Well, you've really put the cat among the pigeons, Mr Metcalfe. I'll have to talk to my boss to see what he recommends. He might want to hear your story for himself. Are you staying in town?'

'I can, if necessary. I'm a free agent and have no other plans.'

'Fine. Do that, at least for today. Where can I contact you?'

'I'm not sure. I'll have to find digs.'

'What about your lady friend? Can't she accommodate you?'

'I haven't asked. I suppose she might.'

'Look, find somewhere convenient then ring me, at the Yard, at three o'clock to give me your address and phone number. Make sure the place *has* a phone, won't you?'

'O.K.' I knew Alison had one. I'd seen it in the lounge with an extension through to that luxurious bedroom.

'Right. In the meantime, I'll speak to my boss and we'll try to find a way of dealing with this little lot. Don't stray far from the phone, will you?'

'What about MacIntyre? What will have happened to him?'

'They'll keep him in custody over the weekend, "pending further enquiries" as they put it. He'll have been refused bail—if they've set up a plot to have him busted, they'll not let him out of their sight. When are the courts held at Richmond?'

'Each Thursday, I think, but they often

hold special courts to remand prisoners either on bail or in custody. They'll keep him in police custody until they convene a special court. He won't have been charged yet which means they can keep him in the cells for as long as they want. But once they charge him with their trumped up crime, he's got to be brought before a magistrate. I think they'll hold him without a charge so their enquiries can be completed, or of course, they could ask the court to remand him in custody for a week at a time. I know how the rural courts work.'

'So he'll be safe from outside harm, they can't kill him under the noses of honest cops,' he puffed at the pipe. 'What about Pierce?'

'Shall I ring the car-park?'

'Forget him. He should be loose now if he's got any lead in his pencil! But he and his mates, whoever they are, will be after your blood, won't they? They'll be convinced that you know more than you really do and, like Thompson, they'll want you eliminated before you do any more harm. I'll have arrangements made to pick him up—and the others if we can find them.'

'What about Alison Jenkins?' I asked.

'She was Thompson's right-hand assistant, so they'll be gunning for her. You'd better warn her.'

'Could they know her address?'

'Yes. We file all possible sources of any security risk of leakage. Her name and premises will be there, among our known prostitutes.'

'So Mortimer or anyone could find out where she lives?'

'That's true, so we'll have him arrested too. But only *I* will know that you are there, won't I? And you've got the Walther.'

I smiled. I hadn't handed it over because I'd hoped to retain it for my own protection, and he'd not allowed that fact to escape him. Legally, I needed a firearm certificate to possess a pistol of this type and the law didn't allow certificates to be granted merely for personal protection. Had Megson wished, he had the power to confiscate it, but he closed his official eyes. That alone indicated he trusted me, and was himself to be trusted.

'When you ring me, introduce yourself to me, and to me only, as Bulldog. Say "Bulldog speaking". I'll reply by saying "Sherlock here". And vice versa. We'll be sure we're speaking to the right person.'

'I understand.'

He drained his pint and left the pub. I followed him out and found that my body and legs ached like hell. I'd had no sleep last night and the food, drink and heat of the pub had taken its toll. I could have fallen asleep in that cosy seat, but forced myself to leave. The fresh air drove away much of the drowsiness but the walk back to the flat seemed to be everlasting.

I made it and told Alison my news. I asked if she could recommend a good place to stay, possibly for a night or two.

'Here,' she spread her hands in a gesture of welcome. 'It's all yours, be my guest.'

'What about your ... er ...?'

'I've already cancelled them, I was to have had two tonight. They understand that sometimes a woman doesn't feel well. They're regulars and will return.'

'Thanks. One night may do—and I could do with a good sleep right now!'

'Jump into the spare bed. I've got some shopping to do—I need food and victuals for my guest! Make yourself at home.'

'I've got to ring Megson at three, so I'll have to remain awake.'

'Please yourself. It's all yours, Martin.

Here,' and she tossed a spare key to me.

'Shall I come with you?'

'No, I can look after myself. I'm not exactly new to intrigue and violence.'

She disappeared with her basket and shopping bag, and by constantly splashing my face with cold water and walking around in circles, I managed to stay awake until it was time to call Megson.

'Bulldog speaking,' I used our introduction.

'Sherlock here,' I recognised his voice. 'I've little further news. The boss has been told and he has had to seek audience with higher authority. I'll ring back at five. What's your address and phone number?'

I told him.

'Pierce had managed to free himself. I've checked at the car-park but he hasn't returned to the office, nor has he phoned. He'll be scurrying around his cronies and we've put an all-stations alert out for him, and for Mortimer. He's off duty today and wasn't at home when we checked.'

'Thanks for telling me.'

'Till five o'clock then,' and the line went dead. I stripped to my underpants, had a good wash and collapsed into the silken bed. I was asleep before my head

191

touched the pillow and was aroused by a distant burbling noise, followed by someone violently shaking me. Through bleary eyes I realised it was Alison.

'The phone!' she said. 'You're wanted on the phone.'

'What time is it?' the sleep was heavy upon me as I forced myself from between those smooth sheets. I sat up, rubbing my eyes and blinking at her.

'Five o'clock,' she wore a coat and gloves. 'It should have roused you, standing right next to your ear like that!'

I reached out and lifted the extension set.

'Hello?'

'Sherlock here,' came the distinctive voice.

'Bulldog speaking,' I had a second's struggle to recall our code.

'The boss wants to talk to you in person,' Megson informed me.

'Where? Here?'

'Yes, and he's on his way.'

'How shall I know him?'

'He'll use our code.'

'Have you any further news about Pierce and Riley?'

'Not a whisper.'

'What about MacIntyre?' I persisted.

'The boss will explain everything. Cheers.'

And he replaced the phone. I shouted the news to Alison who was in the kitchen.

'I'll keep out of the way,' she offered. 'They won't want me listening. You'll have to wait for your tea, though!'

She returned to the bedroom to carry on the conversation. 'I'll go upstairs for a few minutes. There's an old lady who likes a chat. She's an actress of years gone by, quite a star in her heyday, by all accounts. I'll return when they've gone.'

And she left, just like that. I got dressed.

The Special Branch man came at quarter past five and had another man with him. We used Megson's little formula and he introduced his colleague as a Mr Gregory of the Security Service. The name of the Special Branch man was Detective Chief Superintendent Horsley who was in his early fifties, round and portly. Beneath his trilby, which he removed on entry, he had a balding head and his clear blue eyes shone like bright jewels behind his steel rimmed spectacles. Gregory, on the other hand, was much younger. I'd have estimated his age at around thirty-five. His hair was thick and bushy, a dirty blond colour, and he wore a neat moustache and beard.

I showed them into the lounge where they settled on Alison's settee and listened to my story. It took a good half-hour to tell and I omitted all the unnecessary trimmings, relating only hard facts. I showed them the brief-case which had been handed to Alison in Thirsk and they took it for safe-keeping, saying it provided evidence of the link between the hotel plot and the aircraft. When they asked for my opinions or suspicions, however, I said I was sure that MacIntyre was innocent of their allegations and that he was being framed for a very dirty reason.

Horsley agreed.

'Yes, Mr Metcalfe, he is totally honest and as straight as an arrow. I am pleased you have brought this to light. We are now in touch with him, through his wife, and he knows of our interest, and of your part in the story. Mrs MacIntyre is to explain everything on her next visit. We have arranged supervision of Riley and Herriott who are still in Yorkshire, although we are uncertain whether they know of our action at this end. We hope to stop Pierce and Mortimer getting a message to them. A lot of work has been done in the past two hours, Mr Metcalfe, but we are not yet in the clear. Let me give you an example of our current concern—consider the firearm that was used to kill Thompson. It has not been found, has it? I don't think the one in your possession is that particular weapon, so where is it? The woman concealed one under the mattress in MacIntyre's room, didn't she? It would undoubtedly be "found" when the room was searched by Pierce and Riley, and I'm sure that gun killed Thompson. Ballistic tests will give a definite answer. MacIntyre doesn't know the name of the woman who used it, and Riley and Pierce could deny that there was a woman present when they searched the room. Hey presto, MacIntyre is a murder suspect. If we push too hard, I'm sure they'll use that threat.'

'His prints won't be on it,' I pointed out.

'Nor will anyone else's. They'll make sure of that—they'll have wiped it clean. Doesn't that imply guilt by MacIntyre?'

'The girl could testify the truth,' I said.

'If she ever gets the chance. Their intention was to kill her, I'm sure of that, and it could even be possible to frame him for her death too! Remember, only Thompson knew her real identity, so who, on MacIntyre's side, could locate her? They'd already disposed of Thompson.'

I could see why Thompson had insisted on her using her own car—that action alone made her traceable. Had he foreseen this?

Horsley continued, 'I think Thompson saw the light at the last minute and left the woman open to identification, just in case he was right in his beliefs. And he was, to his credit; they feel he's told some of his secrets to Miss Jenkins and I'm sure Pierce was about to kill her for that reason. You can see your problem, Mr Metcalfe! Your life is now at risk. For me, I've got to compel that group of left-wing bastards to drop their allegations against MacIntyre and to forget the pornography charges or whatever else they've got lined up for him. That would be comparatively simple if it wasn't for the murder charge that could be levelled at him instead. We could have words with the local police but we don't know who we can trust up there. So, somehow we've got to make them free him and we must do it in such a way that they cannot retaliate with that likely murder allegation. Poor old MacIntyre's really at risk, isn't he? They must need his knowledge pretty desperately. I'm sure the missing cash will be hidden in England's name, just to add fuel to MacIntyre's "motive" for murder. It will be sewn up all right, Mr Metcalfe.'

'So what can we do?'

'Not a lot at this stage. It's a waiting game. I'm going to tell you something which will reveal their motive. MacIntyre is in possession of some vital facts about the existence of left-wing extremists in our society. They have infiltrated the unions, the schools, the universities, the factories and even our social life in order to spread their evil doctrines to gullible people. They intend to usurp our society—indeed, they're aiming to undermine all Western society and this can only be achieved by inflation of our currency and undermining our internal discipline. I'm sure you are aware of this. MacIntyre has, for the past five years, been engaged on a fact-finding exercise, the object of which was to locate and name the men behind this conspiracy and to produce concrete evidence of their methods. The Government wanted sufficient evidence for them to take action

197

to remove them from their high positions of power.

'On Monday, Mr MacIntyre is due to attend a meeting in Newcastle-on-Tyne. He is going there to discuss his work with eight other men, and to reveal his facts. Those eight other men are top police officials from the other eight E.E.C. countries. They've been doing similar work within the Common Market and the object of the meeting is to pool their knowledge. They hope to establish common factors, to name international operators or organisations, and to make recommendations to the E.E.C. Parliament. The meeting will last the entire week.'

He paused for breath, then continued, 'No other Englishman knows more about the ways the extremists infiltrate the fabric of our society and this means MacIntyre and his colleagues can inflict incalculable harm upon the movement in Europe. His captors don't want to kill him because they wish to find out just how much he really knows. That knowledge is keeping him alive. Now that we're onto them, he could become dispensable. Perhaps they'd rather kill him than risk him giving his secrets to the other side. We've got to move fast now, and we have a slender lead over them.'

Mr Gregory took over. 'This high-level meeting will compile a report for consideration by each participating nation's Government and by the E.E.C. Parliament as a whole. It will be done with a view to eliminating, or at least restricting, extremists of any kind within our society. It is hoped to gently ease the canker from selected sectors.

'Our man, Mr England, was to be resident at the Cleveland Tontine between two other engagements, *i.e.* the Catterick Conference and the E.E.C. meeting. This was done to conceal his movements and to avoid direct travel between his home and the meeting. His chauffeur drove a decoy car from Catterick, just in case. We had to keep him from the eyes of those who wished to wreck the Newcastle meeting. It seems that Riley and Pierce got themselves assigned to the job of protecting him and their mission is to stop him from going to the meeting and to take him into their custody to be later brain-washed and made to reveal all he knows. All these complicated plans were done to make their taking of him seem correct. It seems that the Danish equivalent of Mr MacIntyre has also been "got at". It may be significant that both these police officers belong to so-called progressive societies, societies where pornography is free for all and discipline is breaking down. It makes one wonder if the infiltrators, in the long term, have achieved this by informing the public of their "rights" as opposed to their responsibilities. Their mouthpiece for this would seem to be various socialist organisations. Another side-shoot of the plot was to cast doubts on the integrity of the participants of that meeting so that their testimony would not hold credence with others. Fortunately, we did have some notion of what was going on and have a method of hitting back at them. Plans are already being made to implement it and I needn't go into the details, Mr Metcalfe. However, there is something we would like you to do for us.'

'Yes?'

'They obviously think that you were planted to foil their plans. They believe we sent you.'

'I can understand them thinking that!' I laughed.

'We'd like you to continue and indeed to reinforce that belief. They're running now but it's far from over. We want you to create a diversion as we put our final plan into operation. Will you help us?'

FOURTEEN

Even before I finished uttering my promise of help, Gregory was outlining his requirements. It seemed there existed a counter-plot about which he would say nothing except that it was aimed at a level much higher than Riley, Pierce or Herriott. My job was to frustrate their immediate plans and my terms of reference were fairly vague. It was made clear that I must ensure that MacIntyre did not appear before a court for any reason; I had to prevent his death and if possible I had to secure his release in time for Monday's meeting. That would have been Thompson's task. I could either steal the evidence or release MacIntyre or both. The likelihood of the murder charge should be eliminated by this counter-plot. It was a pity the local police couldn't be told of the plans but someone may talk; this was a Government-backed operation and was therefore top secret. I was reminded of the Official Secrets Act and the declaration I'd signed upon joining the police.

I was unofficially allowed to retain the Walther and its small magazine of ammunition but was given no documentary authority to aid me in this work. It was made abundantly clear that I could expect no official backing if I was caught—in that, I would be alone and no one would admit responsibility for my actions. There would be a cash payment upon the successful completion of the task, a minimum of £500 was offered and accepted! I had to ring Gregory in person if I needed any assistance and he would be my contact man for the operation. Any queries or requests must be made direct to him. He informed me that other agents would be operating in the area, so help would never be far away.

Calls from Gregory to me would be made by telephone to a suitable number which I had to find. All verbal communications would be prefixed by the words Sherlock and Bulldog as before. In the time allowed for questions I asked about the identity of the dead pilot. He was a professional pilot who had been highly paid for the trip; he had been hired through Herriott for that occasion and would know nothing about the plans against MacIntyre. He was a paid carrier and nothing more; he had been used by the Security Service on many previous occasions and thought this had been another of *their* jobs. For that reason, he had no cause to query Herriott's instructions. This information would not be given to Stokesley Police. They now had his name and address, all that was required for the inquest. The purpose of his trip would never be revealed.

'What about Alison Jenkins?' I asked. 'I must consider her safety.'

'She ought to leave this flat,' advised Gregory. 'She can be completely trusted, by the way. Thompson has used her before, as you know. And we have used him regularly—he thought he was engaged by us on this job but obviously smelt a rat. It cost him his life. He was a good man—his wife will receive a pension from the Government, of course. I think Miss Jenkins will enjoy a trip back to Yorkshire. You are advised to make use of her skills,

Mr Metcalfe. But your home address is too well known to the other side. You'd both be at risk there.'

'I can find a safe place,' I assured him.

'Good. Well, you'll be going tonight, eh? You've only got tomorrow to do your stuff.'

'I could use a few hours' sleep,' I yawned as if to emphasise the point.

'My advice is that you leave immediately,' Gregory spoke quietly but I knew he meant every word. 'Certainly you should go within the hour. That'll give you just enough time to have a meal and to make the necessary arrangements.'

'What's the rush?' I asked.

'We've told the other side about you,' he said even more quietly. 'They've been given a "tip"—they'll be expecting you to do something and will be out to stop you as soon as they can.'

'God! You blokes don't waste time!'

'There's a lot at stake, Mr Metcalfe. The ball's in your court and from now the pressure is on them. They're looking for you already.'

I took a deep breath and found that my heart was thumping faster than normal and more loudly. 'I'll do my best,' was all I could think of saying.

They got up, shook me by the hand and let themselves out. Alison heard them clatter down the stairs and returned to ask if I wanted my tea. I said I'd love it and she resumed that chore. In her tiny kitchen I outlined the latest developments and she took it calmly.

'I wanted to thank you for saving my life,' she moved closer to me and leaving the half-prepared meal, slid her arms around my waist. 'I haven't done that yet.'

'Now?' I heard myself whisper, hoarsely.

She led me to the silken bed and I didn't resist. Tired though I was, I enjoyed her thank you; in fact, I've never been so profusely thanked for anything in my life even though the matter occupied a mere thirty minutes. I followed the experience with a hefty and most tasty meal and we decided to use her car to locate mine, then we'd drive north in convoy.

Before leaving, I rang an hotel in Richmond and we booked in as Mr and Mrs Savage; I said it would be eleven by the time we arrived and the receptionist said it would be all right. I rang Gregory to give him my false name, address and phone number.

I wanted to leave our cars in a suitable place near home, say Leeds, and there hire another to give us the added security of an unknown vehicle. The hire agencies would be closed by the time we arrived in Yorkshire, so we'd have to make the entire journey in our own vehicles.

'Ready, Mrs Savage?' I linked arms with her.

'I'm ready for anything,' she squeezed my arm and we left the flat. She carried a small weekend case and a suitcase; I took the latter from her as we hurried down the stairs.

It was nearly seven o'clock and we'd over-estimated, by half-an-hour or so, the time it would take to prepare for flight. I realised this as a swarthy looking individual materialised from a gloomy alcove on the ground floor and blocked our exit at the foot of the staircase. His hands were stuffed deep into his corduroy jacket pockets and he waited in complete silence, legs apart like some tawdry Western sheriff. I didn't wait to hear him speak. I didn't even give him chance to gauge my reaction or to see if he had a gun. I lashed out with a foot and as he ducked, I swung the suitcase to connect with his left ear and followed with a short, jabbing punch to his belly. He crumpled to the floor as Alison came to my side.

'Take the case,' I thrust it at her and lifted him bodily to his feet. Pausing only to judge distance and aim, I planted a right-handed pile-driver on his chin. It hurt my knuckles but it hurt him a hundred times more as he crumpled unconscious to the floor.

'Is there a back way out?' I asked her.

'I'll show you.'

I frisked him and found a small automatic, loaded; I slid this into my pocket. It would do for Alison.

'They move bloody fast down here,' I said as I caught up with her. 'Give me slow moving Yorkshire life any day!'

'They'll be watching my car,' she reminded me as we scuttled down the metal fire-escape and into the dark paved area behind the basement flat. I retrieved the suitcase from her.

'Just our bloody luck!' I cursed. 'Can we hire a car nearby?'

'There's a garage about ten minutes walk away,' she was running across the flagged area towards the exit gate. We emerged into a long and narrow grassy area intersected with many paths and at each end there was a street lamp. Together, they cast a low light and formed useful shadows.

'Keep to the shadows,' I panted. 'He'll recover any minute and if there are others, they'll have seen your flat lights go out.'

She led me through a maze of back streets and at the garage I discovered we could hire a car. I organised a bronze coloured Ford Capri for a week, flung our cases in the rear and within minutes were roaring along Ladbrook Grove towards the A.5 and eventually the M.1. I'd had to provide my real name at the garage because they wanted to see my driving licence. I wondered how long it would be before our hunters found out. I could always change cars ...

'God knows what sort of parking costs I'll be running up!' I laughed as I thought about my own car, somewhere in London, but was relieved that we were under way. 'I'll have to arrange another trip down here with a barrow full of money to collect it!'

'You can always make it an excuse to visit me,' she smiled happily and our

208

conversation became relaxed and cheerful, a chat between friends. I was sure we weren't followed; maybe that villain was alone, maybe his colleagues had waited just a little too long for him to re-appear or maybe I'd hit him harder than I'd intended. It didn't matter—we were free.

Just before entering the M.1, Alison offered to take the wheel and I climbed into the rear seat to catch up with some sleep. It was quarter to eleven when I roused. The car was bouncing over the cobbles of Richmond's ancient market place and I was cold and stiff. She shook me gently, thinking I was still asleep.

'Come on, lazy bones. We're in Richmond,' her voice was calm. 'It's a lot smaller than I expected, much smaller than Richmond in Surrey.'

'And prettier! Thanks for getting us here.'

'You were snoring!' she laughed. 'I didn't think you were the snoring type.'

'Snoring? Me? Never! I don't snore. I'll bet it was something wrong with the car. The back axle perhaps needs greasing ...'

'It was like someone sawing logs! And you writhe about the whole time.'

'So would you, cramped and cold in a

space like this! How some people manage to make love in the back seat of *any* car is beyond me!'

'You need educating, my man. It's even possible in a mini-car. I'll teach you one day ...'

'Come on, Alison!' I was wide awake and sought the door handle. 'Let's get into the hotel and we'll find a cosy bed where you can teach me all you know. It's the King's Head, the big place on the corner over there.'

I'd once stayed here with Julie; we'd taken off for three days, leaving the children with their grandma and we'd used this hotel as a base to enjoy the peace and solitude of Swaledale. Tonight's visit was under very different circumstances and promised anything but peace and solitude!

Our room, with its pale green decor, was on the second floor and had its own bathroom. It overlooked the Market Place and compared with Alison's silken paradise, it was simple or even positively plain, although we had to admit it was cosy and practical in the traditional North Yorkshire fashion. Comfort with no unnecessary trimmings.

I wanted a shave but had no razor and

hadn't thought to buy one, but I stripped to the waist and used the miniature cake of hotel soap to freshen my face and body. I could use a drink too, so after Alison had done her face and hair, we went down to the bar. Being residents, we were not subjected to the rigid liquor licensing laws and I had a lovely cool pint of bitter while she settled for a brandy and dry ginger. She'd earned it.

We adjourned to a quiet corner where I enjoyed the atmosphere of warmth and silence; I bought two pickled eggs, two packets of crisps and two bags of salted peanuts, and they formed a scanty but tasty evening meal.

'You're very quiet,' she said after I'd settled down to eat.

'I'm wondering how to tackle my job,' I crunched a crisp or two.

'Do you know the police station where MacIntyre's kept?'

'Oh, yes. I've been there many times. It's a Divisional Headquarters which means it's manned for twenty-four hours a day. At night, there'll be a skeleton staff. Yorkshire market towns, such as Richmond, are very sparsely policed, you know. I've known Richmond have only one policeman in the office and one out on foot in the town for the whole night. That's from ten o'clock at night until six in the morning. There's usually a panda car patrolling the rural areas, checking isolated shops and post offices, but it's not enough to cope with anything big.'

'Do you know where the evidence against MacIntyre will be kept?'

'I've a good idea. There's a cupboard and a safe in the C.I.D. offices.'

'I'll help, you know. You *will* let me, won't you?'

'If I need you, I'll ask,' I assured her. 'But we need outside help first.'

'Do we? What are you going to do?'

'My first job is to create a diversion—and a hell of a big one. While the police are running around in a flap, I'll break into the station, collect the evidence and free MacIntyre.'

'That will take time and you'll need more than time if you're hoping to achieve all that. Anyway, they'll be expecting you, won't they? They'll all be on full alert—I know how those bastards in Security operate. By now, Herriott and his pals must know you're onto them and might be expecting you to do something. The truth about Pierce may not have filtered to them, but we can't be sure. If you stage your diversion, Martin, I think it will be anticipated. If so, they'll have arranged extra precautions, won't they?'

'My diversion will involve the local police, not Riley and his mates.'

'Martin,' she came closer. 'They have the local police on their side, remember. The local police will not have overlooked the possibility that there'll be plans to spring MacIntyre—they'll know he's likely to be got at because Herriott's lot will have told them.'

'I realise all that, Alison, but I've got to stage a diversion, haven't I? There's no alternative if I'm going to break into the bloody police station!'

'How about two diversions?' she smiled cheekily, looking at me over the rim of her glass.

'Two?' I repeated. 'How the hell can I fix two?'

'What time did you plan to raid the station?' she sipped her brandy.

'In the early hours of Monday morning—two o'clock or thereabouts.'

'It doesn't leave you much time to arrange things. You've only one complete day. Have you any contacts up here?'

'There's a rogue in Thirsk who owes me a favour. It's five years since I saw him. He's handy for this area. He might help.'

'What do you want him to do?'

'I'd like him to stage a post office robbery in Swaledale.'

'On a Sunday night? There won't be much cash in the place, will there?'

'That's not the point, is it? We need a diversion, that's all, not a serious crime. Besides, the place I've got in mind is a combined grocer's store, general factotum and village post office. You can buy anything from postal orders to pop-corn, by way of paraffin and pills.'

'And your second diversion?'

'I hadn't got around to that.'

We discussed the basics of my initial idea and I explained the possible action the police would take if it happened. I wanted a man-hunt, a hue and cry. I wanted the raiders to make sufficient noise to arouse the local people whom I hoped would raise hell. On the other hand I wanted no one to be hurt, but whether or not my robbers kept any of the takings was a matter for their own conscience. I knew the police would turn out in force for a man-hunt; for a routine burglary they'd simply despatch a couple of detectives or even a solitary panda car to take the necessary statements and a list of the stolen property. But for a man-hunt, there'd be police dogs, umpteen vehicles, a mobile radio control point and all the fuss associated with a major operation. I hoped my would-be operator was sufficiently skilled to execute the raid and to lead his hunters a merry dance across the hills in such a way that he avoided recognition or capture.

Alison thought it was a good idea; it wasn't particularly original but it seemed to be practical. It meant a drive to Thirsk to interview my proposed assistant if he was still around, and that must be done tonight. He'd need time to make his arrangements.

For our secondary diversion, I needed a like incident, something which would put a severe strain on all the police personnel and their resources. In an average city, the police can cope with an outcrop of such simultaneous incidents, but few rural police stations are equipped either in numbers or equipment to deal with more than one large incident at a time.

The snag was that I wasn't equipped

either! I wasn't even sure I could succeed with one, let alone two! Alison, God bless her, made a suggestion.

'I could complain of rape,' she said with every indication of seriousness. 'If I stagger into the police station, with torn clothing and tear-stained countenance, to complain I've been de-flowered by two brutal soldiers, that should keep 'em busy looking for the villains who violated me.'

'I may need you for other work—but it's a good stand-by.'

'What you really need is a riot,' she laughed. 'Something big and noisy, right in the town centre.'

'That would be ideal—a Grosvenor Square job—a crowd of turbulent and riotous people, with one violent and common aim.'

'Why not?' she put calmly. 'It's been done before.'

'You've arranged a riot?'

'Yes. We fixed one, me and Paul Thompson. In Doncaster.'

'Alison, are you with the Security Service? They trust you and you know a hell of a lot about fixing things!'

She smiled and kissed me. 'I'm a woman of ill-repute, Martin. That's all.'

'Enough said. Go on—how did you fix the riot?'

'Luck was on our side, I must admit, but we made good use of it. It was a Saturday a few years ago and Sunderland had been playing Crystal Palace down south. It was a cup tie, I think, and we waited until the match had finished. Sunderland won, so we rang the ground at Crystal Palace and Paul pretended to be Chairman of Doncaster Licensed Victuallers Association. To celebrate the victory, he said, the Sunderland fans would be welcome to stop in Doncaster on their return journey, when every pub would supply two free pints between 8 p.m. and 9 p.m. to every man (and woman) holding Supporters' Club membership cards. The chap at Crystal Palace football ground broadcast the message over the tannoy as the fans were leaving and eight bus-loads of thirsty fans descended on Doncaster that night. Every man expected a free drink or two. There was hell on when they found out it was all a hoax!' and she laughed happily at the memory. 'We had our riot. If Sunderland had lost, there'd have been an offer of free drinks to drown their sorrows.'

'There aren't any matches tomorrow,' I sounded dejected. 'Besides we're not on a main bus route either.'

'But there is a garrison of soldiers on the doorstep, isn't there?' was her cool reply.

FIFTEEN

Having accepted that the resident strength of Catterick Garrison would not be large due to it being Sunday night, we did feel confident in our ability to muster at least fifty thirsty soldiers. Many thousands are stationed there. We would have to make our invitation sufficiently early to catch them before they departed elsewhere but at the same time we would have to make sure our guests had only just enough time to drive the five or six miles before the time of the 'offer' arrived. If we had them entering the pubs in small numbers before the commencement time, they'd learn it was all a hoax, word would get around and our riot could degenerate into a damp squib. We settled for nine o'clock; at approximately ten minutes to nine, one of us would ring the C.O. or the adjutant or even the orderly officer, to have our request relayed over the tannoy system. We'd need to know the name of the Chairman of the local branch of the Licensed Victuallers Association and that would be easy to obtain. Any pub would tell us.

Having decided to use this method as our secondary tactic for distracting the police, we would have to re-time the proposed raid on the post office to make it occur a few minutes before the riot, and we'd have to bring forward the time of my raid on the police station. Instead of the 2 a.m. timing, we'd have to plan it to take place during the upheaval in town—say nine-thirty.

This shouldn't present us with too many problems except that at that time of night there would be more policemen around; the night shift starts at ten o'clock, too late for our purpose. We did consider a 10 p.m. start to our soldiers' revelry but by that time most of them would have left the barracks anyway and our opportunity to stage the riot would have disappeared. Upon reflection, however, I realised that the strength of the local police force wasn't all that great and I felt that a nine-thirty catastrophe would be successful.

It was after midnight when we concluded our plotting and I had yet to visit my contact. I was tempted to procrastinate— there was always tomorrow—and an added attraction was the warm bed and lovely woman that awaited me. But I could not delay making contact with Steve Moore. I told Alison I must leave now.

'Where is this man?' she asked.

'Thirsk,' I told her. 'It's about half-an-hour's drive.'

'Can I come?'

We obtained a late key from reception and arrived in Thirsk at quarter to one. The town was gloomy and silent and its market place deserted, a far cry from two or three years earlier when this tiny town was the overnight stop for countless heavy goods vehicles. The new A.19 by-pass had removed that problem and today Thirsk is quiet and rural in appearance. Its cobbled market place has been renovated, the clock pillar cleaned and floral displays add a touch of colour to the town centre.

Moore used to live on the Hambleton housing estate; I'd been there many times in the past and had no difficulty finding his parents' council house. Leaving Alison in the car, I went to the door and began to hammer noisily. Policemen tend to knock on doors as if to raise the entire neighbourhood but it took a long time to produce a reaction here. Eventually a bedroom window did open and there appeared a woman's head, prickly with curlers.

'What's going on?' she slurred her words through toothless gums.

'Is your Steve in?' I called back.

'Who is it?'

'Tell him it's Metcalfe.'

'He doesn't live here any more.'

My heart sank. 'Where does he live?'

'Northallerton. On that new estate.'

'Which house? It's very important.'

'Are you the police?'

'No, it isn't, Mrs Moore. I'm an old friend and I've got to see him urgently.'

'He's going straight now he's married, you know. He's not pulling any more jobs, not with two bairns to feed and clothe.'

'I just want to see him, that's all, and it's urgent.'

She told me his address; it was a private estate, much to my surprise, so we tore across to Northallerton, a ten minute drive.

Steve going straight, eh? It seemed he *had* mended his ways because the house was a small semi-detached with a neat garden and a well-scrubbed appearance.

'Come with me,' I suggested to Alison. 'I might need a woman's touch here.'

The chiming door bell hadn't a hope of rousing him, so I battered on the door with my clenched fist. The din produced a light on the landing and in seconds Steve Moore opened the door to me. He was dressed in pyjamas and his hair was long and tousled. He blinked in the light of his hallway and shivered as he confronted me.

'Yeh?'

'It's Metcalfe, Steve. Martin Metcalfe.'

'Who?'

'Metcalfe,' it had been five years but I thought he would have rememberd me. He clearly didn't for he just stood, blinking and hugging his arms about his chest.

'I used to be a copper,' I reminded him. 'I once did you a favour. When you cut your hand ...'

'Oh, yeh. The cut hand ... yeh, I remember. You got it doctored for me. That was great. It was the first time a copper had ever helped me. Sorry I didn't recognise you. It's been a long time.'

He'd suffered a deep gash across the palm of his hand and I'd found him, in the gents of a local dance hall, bleeding like a stuck pig. I'd dragged him to a doctor, who I'd knocked out of bed, and he'd sutured the wound. Steve had cut an artery and the next time I came across him, about a week afterwards, he promised any help I wanted. He was a thorough rogue then, a nineteen years old layabout who spent his time in the pubs, clubs and dancehalls, fighting, whoring and vandalising.

But now?

'You promised to help if I needed anything,' I reminded, not very hopefully.

'Yeh, I remember. What's it you want?'

'Can we come in?'

He looked at me and I saw his uncertainty, but he stood aside as we trooped in. His lounge was simply furnished but clean and well-kept.

'Sit down,' he invited.

'Steve,' I began. 'Before I start, tell me something. Are you going straight now?'

'Yeh. Honest I am. Since the bairns came along, I've got stuck into a good job and I'm on good money. I've got myself a smashing wife and this ...' and his sweeping hand indicated his belongings.

I glanced at Alison who realised we were on a loser, then returned my attention to him.

'I'm sorry I came, Steve. I wanted you to do a job. I didn't realise how you'd changed. You've done well for yourself.'

'I haven't changed really, Mr Metcalfe. I never did anything vicious, did I? When you knew me? I was just a stupid youth, always fighting and that. I did a few thieving jobs as you know, but I never harmed anyone. Not really. Then I met Sylvia and well, I settled down. I'm twenty-four now. It's time I grew up. Anyway, what was it you wanted?'

'I wanted you to help us to do a job. It's very important but carries a lot of risk.'

'Risk? What sort of risk?'

'Prison. If you got caught, you could get sent down and I couldn't stop that.'

'Sorry, Mr Metcalfe. I daren't. Not that ...'

'No, after seeing how you've settled down, I wouldn't ask you. You've too much at stake and I'd rather take the risks myself. Come on, Alison. We'll let Steve get back to bed.'

As we rose from the settee, his wife called from upstairs.

'Who is it, Steve?'

'It's Mr Metcalfe, love. I'll tell you all about it in the morning.'

'It's not trouble, is it?'

'No, love, it's nothing to worry about.'

He smiled ruefully at me. 'She always worries about me, she thinks I might go back to my old ways, Mr Metcalfe. Look, what sort of a job was it you wanted? It's not to break the law, is it?'

I nodded. 'It's a burglary, but we didn't particularly want anything stolen. It's to create a fuss, that's all. I want to make the police organise a chase, that's all.'

'Why? It's a funny thing for you to do, Mr Metcalfe!'

'It's a funny world we live in, Steve. There is a very important reason, believe me, and it's very involved. But I am on the side of the law and on the side of the police, although the local police know nothing about it. I'm not allowed to tell you any more,' I added the final words as if they explained everything.

'And what's in it for the burglar?'

'Whatever he gets out of the job. I can't offer anything, except silence.'

'You wouldn't have come if it wasn't very important. I've enough brains to realise that. I can't do it—I daren't. But I do owe you a favour and I know two chaps who'll do it, Mr Metcalfe. Tell 'em what you need and they'll fix it.'

'I want no violence, Steve.'

'Fair enough. Look, sit down again. I'll get dressed and take you round to the house. They'll only do it if I ask them.'

He guided us to a car-park in town from where we walked through one of the many alleys that lead off the High Street. Tucked into a corner of one of them was a tiny house, a two-up and two-down type with a dingy appearance.

'I'll do the talking,' offered Steve. 'They are called Eric and Bill Kennedy. Father and son. Bill's the dad.'

He knocked on the door and a dog with a high-pitched voice began to bark. Soon a stooping man opened the door, he was dressed in a pair of grey trousers and a thick shirt, but had bare feet.

'Now, Bill. It's Steve Moore.'

'Who's that with you?' he studied us carefully.

'Friends,' Steve said.

'It's late,' the old man blinked at us, his dark eyes showing black in the dim light. 'You got me out of bed.'

'I know. It's important. We want a job doing.'

'Come in.'

It was one of the tiniest rooms I'd ever been in, with an old black-leaded fire-grate containing the dying cinders of a recent fire. It was cosy and warm, full of worn furniture which most of us would have thrown out but which might realise a small fortune in an antique shop. We were invited to sit at the table, it was covered with a green oil-cloth and bore unwashed supper pots and the remains of a meal. The little dog, a terrier, fussed about our feet. Steve introduced me.

'This is a good friend of mine,' he said. 'His name is Martin Metcalfe.'

'Aye. If he's a friend of yours Steve, I'll see to him. Who's the woman?'

'Alison,' I said. 'She's my girl.'

'I'll go,' and Steve got to his feet, not wishing to become any more involved.

'I'll run you home,' I offered.

'No. I'll walk. It's only ten minutes and besides, the fewer cars there are, the better.' And he was gone.

I shouted, 'Thanks,' after him but don't know if he heard me.

'What do you want, Mr Metcalfe?' asked Bill.

I outlined my proposed burglary to him, without revealing the true reasons, although I did stress the need for a chase and my wish for the incident to be a diversion rather than a genuine crime. He listened, lighting an old pipe as I spoke, and when I concluded he said, 'It has to be near Richmond, eh?'

'Yes.'

'I know just the place. I can fix that, Mr Metcalfe. When do you want it?'

'Tomorrow? I'd like it in the evening, about nine o'clock.'

'We can manage that, me and our Eric.'

'If you get caught ...'

He shook his head and cut me short. 'We won't. If it's a chase you want, I'll provide it. Now, down to the business side of this. What's in it for us?'

'The takings?' I was hesitant. I had precious little cash on me, certainly not enough to undertake this type of bargaining.

'The takings will be nowt, Mr Metcalfe, not in a rural spot like Swaledale. You'll have to do better than that.'

Alison spoke.

'Two hundred pounds,' she said. 'Half now and the balance when the job's done.'

'Three hundred,' his expression never changed.

'Two-fifty,' she countered. 'A hundred now and the balance later.'

'Give me two hundred now and the balance later, and I'll do it for two-fifty.'

'How do I know you'll honour the agreement?' I asked.

'You don't,' he said. 'You've got my word.'

'I trust you,' said Alison and her handbag was open. She produced a wad of notes and counted two hundred onto the green table top, then let him check the amount before tucking them into his rear pocket.

'If I need you, where can I ring you?' he asked.

'The King's Head at Richmond. Ask for Savage.'

'I've got it.'

'If I'm out,' I continued, 'leave a phone number and a time where I can contact you.'

'O.K. Mr Metcalfe. You can rely on me and my lad. I've trained him well. I'll give the buggers a run for their money.

229

Nine o'clock tomorrow night, eh? The job's on.'

'I want no injuries mind.'

'Then there'll be none.'

Our interview was over; I wanted to know how he intended to execute his mission but Alison took my hand and began to lead me towards the door.

'When shall I see you with the outstanding amount?' she smiled.

'Anytime, miss. I'm not tied to a day or two.'

'Shall I fetch it here, to the house?'

'That'll do.'

And we left. As I drove back to Richmond, some fifteen miles distant, she told me I had a lot to learn. She and Thompson had arranged many similar jobs and a thick wad of cash is essential; you hand it over utterly on trust because people like Bill always turn up trumps. In making a deal, one must err on the generous side. I asked about the cash and she smiled, 'A girl's got to earn her living in many different ways, Martin. I'll recover it, so don't worry about that.'

'From Gregory's lot?' I asked.

'Of course,' she smiled.

'You didn't offer it to young Steve?' I mentioned.

'If he'd accepted and got sent to prison, I'd never forgive myself. He's a family man now—you don't ask family men to do this kind of work.'

'That's another lesson I've learned!' I sighed.

When we entered the King's Head, the night porter hailed me and confirmed that I was Mr Savage.

'Yes?'

'There was an urgent call for you, sir, from a Mr Gregory.'

'Yes. What did he say?'

'He asked if you would ring him immediately you come in. He rang about five minutes ago. I checked your room.'

'Thank you.'

He left us as we moved across the foyer. 'It must be important,' Alison was at my side. 'It's not often he rings up like this, after two.'

Using one of the hotel's kiosks, I rang his number and reversed the charges.

'Bulldog speaking.'

'Sherlock here. Listen, Mr Metcalfe. They've kidnapped Mrs MacIntyre, not half-an-hour ago.'

SIXTEEN

The informant, whose identity was not revealed to me, was one of a team who had been maintaining round-the-clock supervision at the MacIntyre home. Tonight, after he'd seen Mrs MacIntyre and her lady friend into the house, he'd patrolled the vicinity as was his practice and had located a car in a field only seventy-five yards from the house. In accordance with his orders, he'd gone to investigate and whilst examining the vehicle, someone had hit him skilfully from behind with what he described as a 'very solid object'.

He'd recovered consciousness a few minutes later to find the car had gone. He'd hurried back to the house to learn that Mrs MacIntyre's friend had suffered a similar attack and that Mrs MacIntyre had been man-handled from her home. All this had occurred about one-thirty and a high level decision, made in London, had decided not to inform the local police at this stage. No description of the abductor(s) had been obtained, the car bore a false registration plate and was probably a decoy anyway.

The Security Service had informed Megson of the Special Branch and it was felt that the outrage had been perpetrated to provide the plotters with a bargaining device, should we succeed in freeing MacIntyre. They would barter his wife's freedom for the freedom of Pierce and Mortimer, both of whom, I was told by Gregory, had now been arrested. So far, no word had been received from the abductors nor was anything known of Mrs MacIntyre's whereabouts.

In trying to anticipate the thinking of their enemies, the Security Service, operating closely with the Special Branch, felt the woman had been taken in the hope that her disappearance would be widely publicised so strict instructions had been given that, on no account, must word of this reach the press or the villagers. Mrs MacIntyre's friend, a lady she'd known all her life, had been partially put in the picture and was now under close guard.

'We have told you, Mr Metcalfe, so that you are fully informed. However, it is not our intention to succumb to any blackmailing threats—we will not release our prisoners even if we receive a demand to do so. I might add that we expect such a demand. Our men, and the Special Branch, will make a detailed search for Mrs MacIntyre—we know most of the homes or hideouts where she may be.'

'How does this affect me?' I put to him.

'It means they're getting desperate. We have brought about an escalation of their plans—everything was geared up for Monday but because we've got some of their operatives in custody, their plans have gone wrong. Monday is now too far away.'

'So they'll try even more desperately to prevent MacIntyre attending that meeting?'

'Exactly. If things had gone their way, it would have been a bloodless coup but I feel desperation is setting in. MacIntyre must be protected at all costs, Mr Metcalfe. We feel his life is now in danger. We know they really want him alive, to bleed him dry of all he knows, but if they get too desperate he could be killed in order to prevent him revealing his knowledge to that meeting.'

'Surely he's put his facts into writing?' I suggested. 'Can't his report be produced?'

'No. We daren't allow him to commit it to paper—paper can be stolen, copied or burnt. I believe he has his store of facts safely lodged in a bank somewhere—only he knows where. That's kept him alive so far. I'm sure. It's vital that he attends that meeting, in person. This meeting, Mr Metcalfe, is vital to E.E.C. trade and industry, as I'm sure you will realise and it will lead to a carefully planned but absolute purge of the extremists and thus end their evil infiltration. He's got to be safeguarded, Mr Metcalfe. His wife is not in any immediate danger we feel, nor was his life until now. They could kill him at any time now—if they do, his secrets will go with him. We won't benefit but neither will the extremists.'

'He'll be safe in the police cells, won't he?'

'Not entirely, not with Herriott and Riley there. No, he's got to be freed. And it must be now *before* we receive any ultimatum from the other side. We've got to be one jump ahead of them.'

'I've already made plans to spring him tomorrow night,' I said.

'That's no good, Mr Metcalfe. You'll have to do it now, *within the hour.*

Thompson would have done it—now it's up to you. You've got Alison Jenkins with you—you'll find she's marvellous at a time like this and a genius when under pressure.'

'Are there any instructions for when he's free?'

'Only that he's got to be safeguarded until Monday—the conference has been arranged to take place in Newcastle-upon-Tyne, but only he knows where. If necessary, he must be accompanied to the locality. That is your new task.'

'I understand.'

'Help will always be on hand, of course, and you will not be alone in this. You are our "front man" as it were and we are depending on you.'

And the phone went dead. I found myself shaking with nervousness and excitement—it had all been so casually dropped into my lap. But the mission seemed so fraught with danger that it was unreal and a far cry from the gentle task of being a country copper. I knew I was being used—I knew I was dispensable; they'd rather lose me than one of their own top men. I was the bait ...

My face must have mirrored my feelings

as I returned to Alison.

'Well?' she was at my side, clutching my arm.

I told her of our ruined plans and wasted time and she accepted the news philosophically.

'This is typical of them,' she told me. 'They always behave like this, expecting miracles.'

'What about the post office raid?' I remembered the little fellow in Northallerton. 'We haven't time to drive down there to cancel it, and there wasn't a phone in his house.'

'Don't worry about that, Martin. We've more important things to consider. Let's get old MacIntyre out first and let old Bill continue with his raid. He'll think he's doing us a favour and besides, it'll be a guide as to his performance and future usefulness. We might want to use him again. Come along, let's go to our room and get started. We've a lot to do.'

We sat on the double bed to make our plans. I knew from past experience that Richmond Police Station was manned, at night, by very few personnel. There was always a constable on duty in the office, a sergeant alternating between the office and town, and possibly in these circumstances, a night duty C.I.D. man on call. The town would have a handful of patrolling constables, probably no more than three or four on foot, and there may be a rural patrol too. That might consist of two or three men in vehicles. That was the normal situation; because of their Very Important Prisoner, there might be additional duty members but I guessed this may consist of a solitary additional constable whose duty would be the welfare of the prisoner. Herriott and Riley would undoubtedly be there, or possibly one of them would remain on guard as the other rested elsewhere. They'd never let MacIntyre out of their sight.

I must not lose sight of the possibility that Herriott and Riley would be expecting a visit but hoped they wouldn't anticipate one as soon as this. I wondered how much of this very personal worry they had passed on to the local police? The local police, I mustn't forget, were of the opinion that MacIntyre was the villain in the affair and that their captors were the goodies. For this reason, I could not approach the police with my knowledge simply because they would not believe me. This meant that our rescue of MacIntyre must be achieved by stealth and cunning, or by violence, or even by a combination of all three.

Both Alison and myself had a firearm and ammunition; as a last resort we might find them useful but I had no wish to fire mine. I'd perhaps wave it at someone but I couldn't see myself pulling the trigger, although Alison told me that you never knew what you'd do if pressed. With my character weakness in mind, I outlined the layout of the station. This would be a passive rescue.

On the ground floor are the operational and supervisory ranks' offices and the cells; upstairs the C.I.D. and administration departments. Leading from the ground floor into the adjoining court room is a passage, the purpose of which is to link the cells directly with the court so that prisoners due for court do not have to be taken outside the walls of either building. This reduces the likelihood of escape. The court house and its satellite rooms and offices are unoccupied at night and although the court buildings are part and parcel of the police station, the entrance to the latter is some distance from the rearmost part of the court. The duty P.C.

would certainly not be aware of anyone creeping around the court, either indoors or out.

We decided that I should enter via the court building. It was the obvious choice. I would break in at the rear to effect entrance to one of the ante-rooms, after which I'd follow the prisoners' passage into the police station. This emerges near the muster room and there are gents toilets, broom cupboards, and miscellaneous offices and rooms nearby. I could readily conceal myself until it was time for my next move.

Leading from the muster room doors, along the length of the ground floor, is a wide corridor at the far end of which lies the Enquiry Office. That corridor runs at right angles to the prisoners' passage, making the building 'L' shaped. The main doors of the police station are used by police and public alike and open on to a counter in the wall of the Enquiry Office. It is behind that counter that the duty policeman works. He keeps the cell keys, or rather they are kept in that office. Half-way along the main corridor, on the right as I would be looking along it, is a side entrance which leads into the rear yard and garages. That would be my escape route.

From a hiding place in the empty and dark muster room end, I would be able to maintain a watch on the counter and to spy on the duty officer. After a good deal of rapid discussion, Alison and I decided to rely heavily on an allegation of rape upon Alison. This was bound to result in something of a flap and it would usefully employ the duty personnel. If possible I wanted her to lure the police outside and to retain them there for as long as possible. I suggested she tell them that her car had been rammed and damaged. This had forced her to stop whereupon two soldiers had jumped out of the other car, dragged her into a field and raped her. She could take our hired car to the station—we would damage it before-hand—and it would also provide us with a get-away vehicle. She must leave the keys in the ignition and describe her attackers' vehicle so that a hunt would be mounted.

She was to allow me ten minutes after effecting entry to the court; after that lapse of time she must drive into the police station car-park. I'd be able to watch her at the counter and when she

241

coaxed the officer outside I'd rush into the office, take the cell keys from the keyboard, release MacIntyre, re-lock the cell and the entrance to the cells. I'd have to ignore the evidence which I'd originally intended to seize—the safety of MacIntyre was all that mattered. I'd keep the cell keys because that would frustrate any attempts to discover whether MacIntyre was still there and if I was lucky, he wouldn't be missed for some time. Prisoners are visited or checked every half-hour during their time in police cells.

I'd take him out of the station by the side door. This can be unlocked from the inside and is always locked at night. We could conceal ourselves in the shadows as we circumnavigated the building to regain access to the waiting car and when Alison had gone back inside to make her formal statement (for which a policewoman would be called from her bed), we would hurry to the car. She must then make an excuse (or several excuses depending upon our progress) to return to her car for a handkerchief, handbag or something. Then we'd all drive like hell from the place.

It sounded too simple but a simple plan is often the best. I went over it, realising that there were many weaknesses. One was the location of the cell keys. If there was very strict security, the keys may be in the possession of a selected officer and not left hanging in their usual place. Another problem was timing—how long would it take me to unlock the cells, rouse MacIntyre, get his shoes on and persuade him that I was on the level?

Then I had to lock up after myself and hustle him from the building. I mustn't overlook the fact that other people may be in the building too and I daren't sit exposed in the waiting car with MacIntyre at my side as I waited for Alison. I'd attract too much attention; a pip on the horn for her? I agreed to this—a double *pip-pip* to let her know we were there. The noise could come from any car ...

I reckoned I'd need a good five minutes and didn't think it would take the constable that long to inspect the damage to the car. Somehow she must detain him outside for as long as possible.

But time was running out. This seemed to be our only viable plan and we were left with little alternative. If everything worked as we hoped, we would be some distance from the station before the alarm was raised. If we failed, or had to resort to guns, there'd be a chase. If Herriott and Riley were involved in that chase, MacIntyre's life would be at grave risk. They could say they'd shot an escaping prisoner.

Our discussions had taken half-an-hour; Gregory wanted him free within the hour. That left thirty minutes.

We left the hotel again, saying 'Goodnight' to a puzzled porter and said we'd soon return. I climbed into our car, drove up the hill towards the police station and found a convenient stone-pillared driveway which led to a private house. I rammed the front offside of the car into one of those pillars and suitably buckled its wing, smashed a headlight and crumpled the bumper. That was our 'rape damage', enough to fool a policeman until the forensic lab. said the damage had been done by a stone and not by metal! But that would take days. I drove to within a hundred yards of the police station and parked nose-first into the drive of another private house. That would rescue the possibility of an unwelcome police check of the vehicle, a distinct possibility at this time of night in view of its damaged state had we left it on a road.

We rapidly rehearsed the story she must tell and I opened the door.

'Five minutes to get into the building,' I said, 'and ten after that. Check watches.'

I left her in the passenger seat, planting a kiss on her lips before departing.

'Good luck,' she whispered.

SEVENTEEN

I climbed the final part of this steep hill from where I could see the silhouetted outline of the police station complex; viewed from this side there appeared to be no lights but this was the rear, the part through which I intended to enter. All was in darkness there, but the front would be illuminated and occupied.

I approached on the open road until the court house was on my immediate right; one of its windows overlooked this part of the hill. It was in a small and informal court room, one used for juvenile hearings which had none of the traditional atmosphere or appurtenances of a court but which was a plain room containing tables and chairs. That window, large and of plate glass, was about six feet from where I stood panting slightly from the exertion of the steep climb. I couldn't hope to break in here because it was so close to the road.

I climbed over the railings and dropped into the surrounding pasture of rough grass and in the darkness began to move along the southern wall of the court house. I moved with intense stealth, ears striving to catch any hint of surveillance and all senses alert for the slightest indication of trouble. At the moment, an old car turned off the Darlington road and began to climb up the hill, so I dropped to the ground hardly daring to breathe as its twin beams swept the area about me. Thankfully, it continued its climb and disappeared over the brow. I heard the changing of its gears as it accelerated into the unseen distance. With my heart thumping, I continued the circumnavigation of the court house, edging past fall-pipes and examining high windows until I came to a corner. The wall along which I had made my way turned a corner and led into an area bounded by two more walls—an open 'square'. To my right was the police station; now on my left was the court house and ahead of me, forming the far wall of this cosy corner, was the passage linking the two. I stood where a fourth wall would have made a square of this area, a square with walls about ten feet long.

It was here, tucked around the court house wall, that I found a suitable window. Round there, I was out of sight from the road and found that it was a toilet window, some six feet from the ground. It was locked.

There is only one way to quickly open a secure window and that is to smash it. With my handkerchief wrapped around the butt of my Walther, I struck the tough pane near the brass catch and froze as the shattered glass tinkled to the ground. To my nervous ears it sounded like an explosion; in fact it was like someone dropping an empty beer bottle and I waited to see if it produced any reaction. I was ready if it did! The duty constable would be at the front, listening to his police radio, dealing with phone calls or typing his reports, and that was a good twenty-five yards away, beyond many walls. He shouldn't hear it.

I waited for what I considered to be a reasonable time before I reached up to release the catch. It was difficult—from where I stood the window ledge was a good six feet from the ground and the catch another foot above that. I had difficulty exerting the necessary pressure and in the end, I had to tap it free, once more using the covered butt of the automatic. This didn't make a lot of noise and when the catch fell free, the window opened easily. It was the work of a moment to pull it wide and after putting away the Walther, shaking bits of broken glass from my handkerchief and brushing slivers of it from the window ledge, I stretched inside to grip the stonework.

I managed to find one or two slender footholds and by sheer dogged determination, I clawed my way inside and dropped, headfirst, into a gents' wash room. Once inside, I pulled the window shut but didn't fasten it. I may need it as an escape route.

For the next minute or so, I had difficulty finding my way around. I had no torch and in here the light was almost non-existent, but as my eyes became accustomed to the gloom I could gauge the size of this small place and saw the outline of the door. I opened it and went out.

I was in a corridor where I turned right and trotted along a passage which was the one used by the prisoners. At the point where it entered the police station there was a barred gate, a massive iron affair which completely closed off the route if necessary, and my heart missed a few beats because it was closed. My way into the police station seemed to be completely blocked.

I approached the fearsome barrier and seized two of its stout uprights—and with a couple of squeaks, it opened! Thank God! It settled back against the wall as I padded through and then, with more oil-less squeaks, it swung back to its original position where it clanked to a halt. I froze ...

The noise echoed along that lonely corridor and must have been heard! It seemed loud enough to rouse the dead and I pressed myself into the dark cavity it occupied when open. I waited for what seemed an eternity but no one came to investigate the din. I began to grow concerned about the time this trek had taken me; I seemed to have been an age getting only this far and was sweating in spite of the chilly night. I wiped my hands down my trousers before entering the police station and stopped to take several deep breaths to calm my nerves before going any further. Ahead was a dim glow, a reflection of the Enquiry Office lights and it was sufficient to guide me over the final yards.

I concealed myself near the foot of the nearest staircase and listened. At this end of the building there was total silence and almost total darkness. All the nearby rooms were unoccupied. At the distant end from where the light came, I could hear low voices interspaced with long periods of silence and realised it was the force radio passing and receiving intermittent messages.

I stole from the shadows to take a look, knowing that I would be unseen in the all-embracing darkness. If you look from light into darkness, you see nothing, a fact well known to patrolling policemen. From this safe position, I could watch the Enquiry Office and the counter. I moved into the centre of the corridor, making sure I had a dark background, in this case a navy blue door, but I was ready to dive into one of the rooms or corners should anyone appear. I looked at my watch. It was twenty-past three and with horror I realised that this was the time the night beat patrols could be in the station, having their meal-break. They usually came at varying times, starting at 1.45 a.m. and continuing to arrive until around 2.30 a.m. Each man took 45 minutes for his break and the times were staggered to avoid all the men being in the station at the same time. Generally, the latest came in at 2.30 a.m. which meant he should leave at 3.15 a.m., but lots stayed on for a chat. I know I used to! I had no idea how many men were on patrol in the town tonight and would have taken steps to find out if I'd been given adequate notice of this mission. But it was too late now—I just had to hope that none lingered here.

From my vantage point I watched the Enquiry Office and the counter to which the public comes for advice, but could see no police officers. I guessed that he (or they) would be seated at a desk, writing or reading or just talking. And all the time, in the background, the radio burbled.

I could only wait; surely my ten minutes had elapsed? Alison must be here soon. I was helpless until she arrived.

More long minutes passed and I was growing fidgety and nervous and then I heard the opening of the front door. It crashed home and was followed by solid footsteps. A police sergeant appeared and my heart sank. He crossed the corridor, moving past the counter and disappeared through a door on my right. He reappeared behind the counter and I saw the constable stand up to talk to him. I couldn't distinguish their words but was able to hear their indecipherable conversational buzz. There appeared to be no other person in that office and I was confident that the remainder of the station was unoccupied, apart from MacIntyre who would be asleep in the cells.

'Come on, Alison!' I whispered. 'Get moving.'

But she didn't come. I checked my watch. Twenty-seven minutes past three. It was over fifteen minutes since I'd left her. Had I been wrong to trust her? Had she had a last minute touch of nerves? Had she been found by a policeman in town? All sorts of calamities flashed across my waiting mind. I'd give her another minute. One full minute and then I'd *have* to act. I daren't wait any longer; the seconds ticked by and I watched the pin-point of light which was the second hand of my watch.

Suddenly there was a commotion outside. I heard the screeching of car tyres, a blaring horn and lights flashed across the counter and far walls of the corridor. It jerked the men into action and two heads peered through the Enquiry window as, outside, a woman's voice was raised into a long series of high pitched screams.

If this was Alison, she was really going to town! Her screams would rouse half the neighbourhood. I tensed myself for action, heart thumping as I listened for clues as to the next stage in the drama. A car door slammed and more screams sounded outside; by this time the two policemen had stirred themselves into action and were running from their sanctum. They crossed the corridor and I heard the outer door crash home as they hurried to investigate. I ran too. I prayed that it *was* Alison and that she'd keep them outside for a few minutes. I wanted time to unlock the cells. As I neared the office door I heard a woman sobbing outside. I had to pass those outer doors and I trusted that all their attention would be riveted upon the mystical female.

As I dashed past, I caught a glimpse—it *was* Alison. I recognised her clothing. She was sprawled across the bonnet of our car, sobbing, crying and beating her fists upon it. Its engine was running, I noted; I saw the two figures close to her showing evident concern but apparently uncertain as to their action. I took this golden opportunity to slip through the side door that led into the office.

I knew where to find the cell keys. I'd been here before, occasionally with prisoners, and found the keys in their usual position on the keyboard. The young office constable had committed an unforgivable sin—and his sergeant had condoned it. They'd left the office unattended and worse still, had allowed unauthorised access to their very important prisoner. Alison's role was beyond reproach and now it all rested on me.

I had the key and went to the door in the corridor of the office. This led into the cell passage and was locked. It was kept locked when the cells were occupied and I slid the key into the lock. It swung open with a hollow sound—the same key also fitted each cell door. Inside the cell passage was a dim light from a low-burning bulb in the roof, so I pushed the outer door home but left it unlocked. I did consider locking myself in to give me time to cope with MacIntyre in absolute safety, but if we were to make a dash for freedom, those precious seconds spent fiddling to unlock it, and the noise it would make, would attract anyone in the office. It was not worth the risk.

My location of his cell was an easy matter. It was first of the row and a dim light burned inside. The others, whose doors were ajar, were in total darkness and I automatically adopted the routine police practice of peeping through the spy-hole in the solid door.

Mr MacIntyre was asleep on his rough cell bed and he was alone. His shoes were outside and I knew that all belts, braces, ties and anything else by which he may harm himself would have been removed. That's why his shoes were outside the cell—he might use the laces to harm himself or the shoes to attack his gaolers. These precautionary measures are adopted for all prisoners in police cells.

In here, I could hear nothing of events outside, consequently I had no idea of

Alison's progress; I put the cell key in the lock and turned it. It unlocked the door with a solid 'clunk' and I pushed it wide open. MacIntyre didn't move nor did he give any indication that he was aware of my presence. I eased the door shut behind me, taking the key from the lock.

'Mr MacIntyre!' I touched his shoulder. He groaned in his sleep and moved uneasily. I tried again. 'Mr MacIntyre.'

I shook him a little more and realised I was treating him like an underling treats his boss! But he wasn't my boss any more. I was too gentle; this time I shook him roughly and slapped his face. It worked. He sat up with a sharp cry and the cell blankets tumbled from him as I clapped my hand over his mouth.

'It's all right, sir,' I fell instinctively into respectful police tones as I addressed him. 'It's Metcalfe. I've come to get you out of here.'

'Metcalfe?' I removed my hand to let him speak. 'Good God! *That* Metcalfe! What's going on?' He was fully awake in an instant.

'I've got to get you out of here. There's a car waiting in the front car-park and we've arranged a distraction to occupy the station personnel.'

His mind was working rapidly. 'My wife mentioned you. You're with Security now, eh?'

'I'll get your shoes, sir.'

I opened the door and brought in the shoes as he slid out of bed; he was fully dressed although he wore no jacket or tie.

'My jacket is at the far end of the cell passage, Metcalfe, hanging near the wash basins.'

He used his police disciplinary tone to me. Metcalfe I'd been all those years, and Metcalfe I was to be now. As he fastened his shoes, I told of the difficulties just beyond the passage door. If they'd brought Alison into the Enquiry Office to be interviewed, it would be impossible for us to leave unseen. We had to leave the cells by that door—there was no other and we'd have to take care of our problems as and when they arose. I told him my plan was to leave the station by the side door once we were out of the cell block. He understood; he knew the layout as well as I. If only there'd been another simple exit from the cell passage! But there wasn't.

Cell passages are built for security—that's the whole idea of having their entrance in a place which is fully manned for twenty-four hours a day.

It took no more than twenty seconds to complete his dress and I ignored his personal belongings. They would be locked in a cupboard, the fate of all prisoners' bits and pieces like rings, watches and coins. They are restored to the prisoner upon leaving the station. MacIntyre may recover his when this was all over.

I crept back to the cell passage door and very gently eased it open, just a fraction, so that I could peer into the office. It was empty! The force radio was babbling on about a stolen car at Guisborough but of the occupants and Alison, there was no sign.

'Come along,' I said. 'They're still busy somewhere.'

We were about to creep out when I heard voices. They were coming back; I heard the office door crash open and that meant we couldn't leave. We'd meet them in the main concourse ...

'Wait!' and we hustled back into the passage. I strained my ears from behind that solid door as they came into the office.

I could hear Alison sobbing and wondered about her next move as a voice said, 'See who's on call in the C.I.D. and get the policewoman out. Get Control Room to start a search for those soldiers and their car. Do it immediately, son. Have a word with the Garrison police too. They'll do the necessary there ...'

And poor Alison would have no idea where I was! I would wait a little longer, hoping they'd take her to the woman's room, or to the doctor's room, or that she'd do something for us. The minutes began to tick by and then, right behind me, I heard Riley's Cockney voice,

'Put your hands up, Mr Metcalfe. And you, MacIntyre.'

EIGHTEEN

He'd been in one of those dark, empty cells and I'd never checked! I could kick myself ... I must be as naïve as hell. I might have caught him asleep ... I hesitated before obeying, but he jabbed me in the spine and said, 'Come along,

Metcalfe. You know I'm not bluffing.'

'Do as he says, Metcalfe,' came the quiet voice of Mr MacIntyre. I pulled open the door and it let in some light; my action caused looks of amazement from the office staff but when Alison saw me she gave absolutely no indication that she knew either me or MacIntyre.

'What the hell ...' and the constable's eyes went to the keyboard. Alison, God bless her, began to sob loudly, valiantly playing her part as the victim of a savage assault and totally ignoring the drama about her. We were urged right into the office where Riley spoke to the police officers.

'This is just as I thought, gentlemen,' he looked at me with coldness in his eyes, 'It's an attempt to release Mr MacIntyre—and who is this woman?'

As Alison's face was revealed, Riley recognised her. 'Mrs England, the lady in the Tontine, eh? Alias who? What's her real name, I wonder? She's our feminine plotter—look at her, Mr MacIntyre. This is the woman who held you at bay in that hotel—and this is Metcalfe, the man who has always been so conveniently around and yet who claims he's not involved in anything! These people do not wish to release you for your safety, Mr MacIntyre, their aim is to destroy you.'

I was in the centre of the floor as he rambled on; Riley and MacIntyre were behind me, just beyond the range of my vision; in front was the office constable, the sergeant and Alison who was seated on a chair, gently sobbing. As Riley delivered his piece of patter, she rose from it with a look of abject misery on her face and tears streaming from her eyes.

'I've been attacked, can't you understand?' she cried. 'Two soldiers ... they ... they ...' and she collapsed to the floor in a realistic faint. The constable and his sergeant went to her aid, an instinctive reaction, and I knew everything depended upon me.

'The car!' I shouted at MacIntyre and as I spoke I twisted viciously around to my left with my elbow jutting out. It was intended for the soft part of Riley's body. I could feel him close to me but he'd eased the pressure of his gun during the current upset, but it would still be there. I connected. I heard him grunt with pain and followed immediately with a foul kick to his shins as I dived aside and twisted to face him. The gun was in his right hand but well off target. The two policemen recovered their wits and came to his aid, but Alison was on her feet in a split second and was fumbling in her handbag. The policemen ignored her as I swung punches at them, putting them between Riley's gun and myself. Mr MacIntyre hadn't run to the car; instead he entered the fracas. His two hands were clamped over Riley's gun arm and this prevented the rogue from effectively using his weapon. Both the local policemen came for me, the sergeant with a truncheon waving dangerously close to my head and the constable weaving in like a wrestler. Then Alison's voice calmed us all.

'Stop it, all of you,' she shouted. 'I have a gun.'

She stood on a chair and covered the office. The policemen stopped immediately. I was free. I was interested in Riley who still had his pistol and who was still struggling with the ageing Mr MacIntyre who clung to the gun arm for all he was worth. Riley had missed his opportunity—he could have killed at least one of us.

'Stop it, Riley,' Alison spoke softly now. 'Or I'll kill you.'

He obeyed and I produced the Walther from my jacket pocket.

'Take his gun, Mr MacIntyre; you policemen, get over against the wall.'

As Riley was relieved of his firearm, the two local policemen moved to a convenient space against the office wall where I made them turn their backs to us and removed the truncheon from the sergeant's grasp. I also took the handcuffs from his trousers pocket where I knew they'd be. The office constable carried no such appointments due to the nature of his indoor duty.

I approached Riley and, under Alison's cover, handcuffed his hands in front of his body. I knew that MacIntyre was looking at the woman with apprehension in his eyes and I said, 'She's with us, Mr MacIntyre, I assure you. Riley's the extremists' agent, not Miss Jenkins. I'll explain it all later.'

'Herriott is still at large,' she reminded us. 'They can still cause trouble.'

Riley came in. 'It's too late to stop us now, Mr MacIntyre. We have your wife. You didn't know that, did you? She's our trump card—either you talk, or she dies.'

The ageing man said nothing and I

didn't know if he believed Riley. He went over to the two policemen, still facing the wall, and said, 'When we leave here, sergeant, I want you to report this immediately to your Chief Constable, in person. Ring him directly, will you? If he wants any further confirmation of the honesty of the release, ask him to contact Mr Gregory of the Security Service, will you? Is that understood?'

'Riley is a left-wing subversive agent,' I told the sergeant. 'He is a member of our Special Branch unfortunately, but won't be for much longer, I can assure you. He and his henchmen have been trying to frame Mr MacIntyre for reasons which I can't divulge here. Herriott is part of his plot and must be found too.'

The sergeant didn't know who to believe and who could blame him? I knew the escape would reach the ears of the Chief Constable in any case; the escape of *any* prisoner has to be notified to the Chief. Riley didn't say anything, so I made the next move.

'Let's go now, Mr MacIntyre, before Herriott gets onto our tail. I suggest we take Riley with us, at least for part of the way.'

'Yes, do that. We can dispose of him at a certain police station known to me. It's in County Durham.'

'Right. Let's go.'

I asked Alison if she'd drive and we put MacIntyre beside her in the front passenger seat; I sat in the rear with Riley who was still handcuffed and the astonished policemen watched us leave.

'Don't forget to telephone your Chief Constable,' called MacIntyre.

'Should we have seized the evidence against you, sir?' I asked as we drove away. 'They could still prove a lot against you.'

'No, leave it. It will be taken care of. There are more urgent matters to cope with. Our first task is to dump Riley and if you follow my directions we'll soon achieve that. I will put him well out of the reach of his friends.'

Riley said nothing.

We turned left as we drove from the police station yard, went down the steep hill towards the town centre but instead of turning right into the ancient market place, we took the left turning. From there, he directed us towards the Great North Road and told Alison to head for Darlington.

She drove easily and well, and during the trip no one spoke.

Each had his own thoughts and after half-an-hour I began to feel that Riley was a little too quiet, or even a little too confident. That he had anticipated our raid was beyond all doubt but had he *wanted* us to get away? The fight in the station had not been too strenuous on his part and I knew he could have killed me, if he'd wanted, and probably MacIntyre too. But he'd held his fire.

Furthermore, had the raid been truly anticipated, one would have thought there'd have been more stringent precautions. I'd have expected more men on duty, an awareness among the staff that such an attempt would be made and even firearms in the station. I got the impression that this eventuality had not occurred to the policemen on duty. They'd left that office quite innocently, both of them, and it wouldn't have happened if Riley had warned them of an impending raid.

Riley had known someone would attempt to free MacIntyre. I was sure of that—Gregory had implied as much over the phone. And Riley had been in the cell, waiting, but locked out of MacIntyre's cell.

266

Could he have killed the H.M.I. if he'd really wanted? He could, but he'd have been discovered and caught; he'd have been tried and convicted, but by letting someone else kill MacIntyre, Riley would be able to continue his work of infiltrating the police ...

My mind raced as we continued along the Great North Road without exceeding the speed limit and I began to grow increasingly worried about our journey. I thought of MacIntyre's wife. I wondered what lay in store for us. How 'safe' was the place he intended to deposit Riley. Obviously, Riley and Herriott were not operating alone in this part of the county and their network, due to excellent but unwitting contacts in the police, would be vast. I began to fear that we were heading for a trap—a trap in which MacIntyre might well be the loser. Out here he was less safe than if he'd remained in those cells; he could be 'got at' quite easily. Was that it? Had we played right into their hands? Had we given them MacIntyre on a plate?

We had! Suddenly I saw it all. I'd been a bloody fool!

'Sir,' I addressed him. 'I'd like to stop

at a convenient place, as soon as possible. It's urgent.'

'I'm in a hurry, boy!' he returned. 'Is it important? Do you want a jimmy-riddle or something? There are toilets in Darlington.'

'I can't wait that long,' I decided to use this as an excuse, 'Can we pull into a lay-by before we get to Darlington?' I knew there was one not far ahead.

'Oh, all right. What a time to choose for a thing like that! You're worse than a child, man!'

Clearly he was still my chief constable and I was just a constable under his command, but I had won. I wanted to surprise Riley; I *must* surprise him.

The lay-by in question was just a minute away. A minute is a long time but I had to risk it. It lay just south of Darlington and was used by lorry drivers for their statutory rest periods and by caravanners and other motorists for a leg-stretch or a nap. It was off the Great North Road and I directed Alison to it. Whether we would have gone through the town had it not been for my 'emergency', I don't know, because the new by-pass effectively carries most of the heavy traffic away from the town centre.

We took the turn to Darlington and I kept my eyes open for the lay-by; as we approached, my heart sank. There was a police road-check in operation at that very point and all traffic was being directed into the lay-by.

'Damnation!' I cursed under my breath.

'What is it?' Alison asked with nervousness in her voice. 'They're not looking for us, surely?'

'I doubt it,' I said. 'It looks like a routine spot check. They do this every so often on main roads. They check for such things as stolen vehicles, antiques or cattle, or they look for escaped prisoners or wanted persons hitching lifts.'

I could see the blue rotating lights ahead, two of them. A uniformed police officer was ushering all the travelling cars, a surprisingly large amount for this time of the morning, into the lay-by where they queued for attention. I leaned forward to peer at the scene. Of all the bloody things to happen—just when I'd wanted to search Riley! I should have done so before, at the police station, and that was another slip on my part. The reason for my desire to halt was to thoroughly search him. He may have a radio set; he could well have called up Herriott from the seclusion of his cell to inform him of this break-away. Did Herriott not know where we were heading? I'd not seen Riley make any calls and in any case he was handcuffed, but I knew our Special Branch utilised throat microphones, or mikes concealed in the knots of their ties or elsewhere among their clothing.

'Mr MacIntyre,' I asked urgently. 'Would we have come this way in any case? If I hadn't asked for the halt?'

'Yes, we would. This is the route I intended to use.'

I didn't know County Durham too well but by that fact alone, the police station for which we were heading must lie somewhere in the south-east corner of this small county and probably not far from Cleveland, as the Teeside area is now known.

I turned on Riley. 'These are your boys, aren't they? You *knew*—you wanted us to get caught again, this time by your mob! And if that happens, it's curtains for Mr MacIntyre. Alison—go like hell. Burst through that roadblock!'

'But ...'

'No buts, Alison. Go. Knock one of

them over if need be—they'll give chase
...'

Riley reacted as I'd hoped he would. He shot forward in his seat.

'Don't be a bloody fool, woman! They've got orders to shoot any car that doesn't stop.'

I laughed aloud. 'And they might kill you, eh? Well, I suggest you put your face to that back window, Mr Riley, and let them see just who they're shooting at. Mr MacIntyre, duck down. Get out of sight.'

He obeyed. Alison turned briefly to look at me and I wished I'd been at the wheel, but there was no time to change drivers. They'd know our car; they'd have advance information and Herriott may well have been in Richmond Police Station as we were raiding it. He may have been hidden upstairs, watching and checking every move we made.

He'd know that we had Riley, but was Riley expendable?

My guess was in the affirmative; he wouldn't realise that himself, not for a few more moments anyway! Soon he may die for his bloody cause!

As we approached the blockade, I examined the road ahead. Two police cars were positioned on the main road, each with their blue lights rotating and all other lights on. A man was at the wheel of each car and both faced Darlington, ready to give chase if anyone burst through. A car could get through—was that their intention? To allow us to burst through and use that as an excuse to machine gun us?

In the centre of the lay-by, which was on our left, stood another car also facing Darlington and like the others, this bore a rotating blue light. On the road at our side was a notice saying, *'Police Check Point. Slow down and obey signals'*. Two men, each with fluorescent clothing over their uniforms, stood on the road and a car, just checked, was wending its way to freedom. All vehicles travelling from both directions were being guided into that lay-by to be searched and their occupants examined and questioned. A huge bluff.

'Alison,' I leaned forward and spoke quietly to her. 'Those aren't Durham Police cars. The registration numbers aren't local—the Darlington series are HNs, and Durham is either J, PT or UP. Durham County Council would register all their vehicles locally—that car, on the nearside, is XE. That's a London registration. I think they're fake police.'

We had slowed right down now for there were five cars in front of us, all facing in our direction and queuing to the left of the stationary car in the lay-by.

'We've got to get out of here,' I continued to speak quietly so that any mike he had didn't pick up our conversation. 'Can you drive well enough to tackle it?'

'Yes,' she sounded confident.

'Right. We've lost a lot of speed but I want you to accelerate to the *right* of that checking car, the one in the lay-by. That's *against* the direction of the vehicles being checked, and then pull round, hard right, and come back this way by going between the two cars on the road. There's just enough room to get through—there may be shooting.'

'There will be shooting!' said Riley coldly and with a trace of nervousness.

'They're facing the wrong way to give chase,' I still spoke softly to her. 'We might just make it—if we don't, all our work goes for a burton. They'll kill Mr MacIntyre.'

'They'll kill us all!' Riley's voice rose into an hysterical laugh. 'They'll kill us all, Metcalfe, you bloody fool. You've walked right into a trap. Right in. Up to the bloody neck!'

'Ready Alison?'

'Yes,' but her voice was nervous too. I wanted desperately to have hold of that steering wheel to guide our car through their barrier but she was moving out now. In second gear, she stamped on the accelerator and the Capri responded vigorously, its wheels biting into the tarmac as I shouted, 'Get down ... get as much car as you can between you and them.'

And I slid into the well behind her as the handcuffed Riley did likewise. He was behind MacIntyre, already crouched beneath the dashboard. Only Alison sat upright; that girl was brave. I hated leaving this task to a woman, or indeed to anyone else, but I had no choice now. I felt the car respond; third gear gave us more speed and she was shouting, 'Get out of the way, you bastards. Get away from me ...'

Lights came up ahead; a car was being guided into our lane, it was approaching us and I felt her swerve as the noise of it whooshed past and people began to shout. They were ordinary people, innocent motorists who had been pulled in by fake police, people going on holiday or returning from a late night out. People submitting to this confidence trick and cursing the innocent ...

'We're past the checking vehicle,' she called. 'They're getting ready to chase us ... they're running to the cars! I hope to God none of them have their engines running ...'

Our car rocked and bucked like a coble on a stormy sea as she put all her weight on the wheel, heaving it down to the right and leaning with it as the car tried to execute an impossible turn. The angle was too acute; she had to stop, reverse and leap forward again as the angry citizens shouted abuse at us and blew their horns. Then a loud hailer rent the air with a cry of 'Police, Halt!'

'One of their cars is moving!' she cried. 'It's closing the bloody gap!'

'A car can get through a very small space,' I shouted as I detected a slight deceleration on her part. She mustn't ease off. She mustn't. She didn't.

'You bastards!' she shouted in open defiance and our Capri leapt forward. On our roof I could see the reflected lights, red, blue and white. All flashing. There was the blur of the night beyond, the hiss of wind, the roar of our engine and the crackle of tyres so close to my head.

'I'm going through,' she called. 'I'm going to make it!'

Then she cried, 'God! One of them's got a machine gun!'

NINETEEN

With the exception of Alison, each of us crouched in the depths of that vehicle; as the driver, she had to remain at the wheel in order to bear the rest of us to safety and her head and shoulders were clearly visible, even from my position on the floor. I could feel the power of the car beneath me, the shudder of its wheels as it strained into that acute turn at her command and this was followed by a sickening crunch as we were rammed by one of the fake police cars. Alison was crying; I could hear her shouting, cursing and sobbing above me, vowing hell-fire and thunder against the bastards who dared to stand in her way.

She battered her way between the opposing vehicles; our car slewed aside beneath the first impact and I could hear mens' voices outside, shouting at us, commanding us to halt and, finally, threatening to shoot.

I called, 'Keep it going for God's sake. Keep it going, Alison!'

She did. As we received a second broadside, this time from the car on our right, we slithered into a side movement on the smooth surface but she corrected this, changed down a gear and shot away at a new angle as the car on the left came in again. I saw its lights on our roof; it caught the rear of the Capri and twisted us in our tracks nearly halting our progress. MacIntyre cried out in alarm as we were thrown and battered from side to side, but the power of our forward movement was sufficient to carry us through that moving barricade. We were free.

Then came the shots.

As our tail end continued to wag due to our vicious acceleration, the first barrage of shots came from behind. We could hear them thudding into the rear of our car and I worried about the tyres. Could she cope with a blow-out at speed? And the petrol tank? Two bullets burst with a crack through the rear window and pierced the skin of the roof in their murderous flight. In another chattering barrage, Riley screamed and slumped to the floor, his bulk coming to rest against my back as Alison forced the protesting car to its maximum. She was still crying and swearing as I shouted, 'Lights. Put our bloody lights out!'

Once again, I heard the distinctive rattle of the machine gun, wondered about its effective range and imagined bullets spraying us and our car. Some did; they peppered and pierced the metalwork like thousands of meteorites battering a dying space rocket. This time Alison screamed and slumped forward over the wheel. The car began to career across the road and I leapt from my secure place.

The groaning Riley, who'd been partially supported by my body, tumbled over with a cry and I could feel his weight against my legs as I grabbed the steering wheel. I was able to steer our careering car along that wide open road but had no control over its speed, accelerator or brakes.

Just ahead there was a turning to the left. I know it well for it led to Northallerton. Alison's foot was on the accelerator and I shouted to her, 'Lift your foot. Alison, lift your foot ...'

But we got round. Somehow I managed to guide the screaming vehicle off that main road and we were bolting down a second-class highway and building up speed. She was slumped in her seat and blood was oozing from her shoulder. I felt it hot and sticky on my hand; she was trying to say something as I fought with the wheel. Shots were still screaming at us but we were dropping down a slope, heading towards a point where we would be shielded from them. One or two shells battered our rearmost parts and peppered the bodywork. A lucky one whizzed through the shattered rear window, flew the length of the car and departed through the windscreen leaving a neat, round hole. I expected the glass to shatter but thankfully, it didn't. We were out of their sight now, but the bloody Capri was still bolting like a panic-stricken horse; we were heading for a drop in the road and a sharp bend.

'Can you reach the brake, Mr MacIntyre?' I shouted above the noise of the engine. 'The footbrake?'

'I'll try,' he said weakly.

Alison's body had relaxed; she'd drifted

into total unconsciousness and the car began to slow down as her foot relaxed some of its pressure. MacIntyre, pale and terrified, clambered from the floor and sat upon his own front seat. I waited; for the moment we were free from pursuit but once they got their cars turned around, they'd be on our heels.

'Brake and clutch!' I shouted at him. 'Try to stop the car. Then I'll drive ... they'll be here soon. Take the wheel for now.'

He obeyed me. With trembling hands, he seized the rocking wheel and took control of the car's direction. It swayed slightly as he struggled with the steering and I took hold of Alison. From the rear, I pushed my arms beneath hers, hoping to lift her to one side to allow MacIntyre greater freedom of movement. She groaned softly as the car's forward rush slowed even more and suddenly MacIntyre was in complete control.

'Stop as soon as you can,' I said. 'I want to put her in the rear, then I'll drive.'

I looked through the shattered window behind me and saw lights moving. They were coming, but hadn't reached this side road.

'There's no time to get her out. Move her over to you, sir. I'll help.'

The car came to a halt and I leapt out, not bothering to examine Riley. I opened the driver's door and Alison almost fell out. I caught her and eased her bleeding form towards MacIntyre. He helped me to half-drag the injured girl nearer to his side. Our lights were out but the engine was ticking over. I squeezed in and spoke softly to her. There was no response but she was breathing noisily. She probably had no idea what was happening and I asked MacIntyre to care for her.

I slammed the door and found myself occupying about half of the driver's seat, a most uncomfortable position in which to drive, but there was no time to seek comfort. I let in first gear, put up the lights and took off. I was just in time. As I pulled away, two sets of headlights appeared behind and I accelerated for all I was worth. They would gain on me during those first anxious moments, but once I'd reached top speed I could hold my own with any driver.

I had one object in mind—to evade the hunters. I had a severely injured girl who desperately needed attention. And Riley?

The extent of his injuries was not known to me and now he made no sounds. But I hadn't time to concern myself with him. I gave the car everything it had, and a Capri can certainly move when given its head. The needle crept up to ninety as the wind hissed around us. It whistled through the hole in the windscreen and ruffled my hair. I made full use of the road so that I could corner at seventy and accelerate from each bend to gain precious yards. They never let up either; there were two cars and I watched them in my mirror. They seemed happy to remain about fifty yards behind but apparently had no weapons. They were running me to earth, watching every move I made and would follow me until I stopped, wherever that happened to be.

As I tore through the night, he produced the automatic he'd taken from Riley, checked it and found it loaded, keeping it in his hand.

Northallerton lay ahead. I was rapidly approaching that sprawling town and took the right hander at Great Smeaton almost on two wheels, ignoring the temptation to use one of the side roads leading to Cowton and Richmond. The open road offered greater scope to a car of this sort. Besides, Alison needed treatment and there were hospitals in Northallerton.

Could I lose them in that town? I had no idea who these people were in their vehicles dressed as police cars, but did they know the area? Did they know they'd injured any of us? Would they know I was likely to seek a hospital?

As I tore along the straightening road, eating the final seven or eight miles into Northallerton, my mind was turning over the possibilities open to me. The town was too small to lose them completely, although I did know some of the newer housing estates sufficiently well to give them a merry dance. Two of them might easily corner me, however, in spite of my dodging tactics. MacIntyre must be my first priority and yet I owed much to the brave girl who was wedged between us. I knew where to find the Friarage Hospital—I must lose them before driving into its grounds.

I maintained a speed well over ninety on that long straight run, roaring past the site of the Battle of the Standard which had been fought here way back in 1138. And then, as I roared towards the rail crossing, heaven-sent providence was on my side. It was a barrier-type level crossing and the warning lights were flashing. I checked the mirror. They were still a good seventy yards behind, apparently content to keep me in sight and to be ready for any sudden movement or turn I might make. They hadn't bargained for this; I was streaking towards those barriers when they began to descend.

The lights had changed to red but speed was on my side. I thumped the accelerator to squeeze the last ounce of energy from the gallant car and hit the crossing as the tendrils of the first barrier brushed our roof. MacIntyre ducked instinctively; I'd beaten the first one but smashed into the second to shatter the brittle timber pole into tiny pieces as the bruised car ploughed through the wreckage. I didn't slow down; I knew the train would arrive in seconds; would they dare to make a run for it? The barrier was down ...

They didn't. Even before I vanished into town, they came to a halt at the far side of the solitary barrier as distant thunder of a train could be heard. A huge diesel powered engine and its long train of trucks was bearing down.

Out of their sight, I dodged down Quaker Lane and emerged onto Brompton Road where I turned right and drove like fury towards the Friarage Hospital. In the hospital grounds, I followed the signs to the Casualty Department and screeched to a halt outside the door, rang the bell and with MacIntyre's aid began to carry Alison from the car.

A sister appeared, looking calm as they always do, and I said, 'She's been shot in the shoulder. She's bleeding a lot.'

'Take her in and place her on the trolley,' the sister turned and led the way. We followed and she called a young nurse to wheel away Alison for immediate attention.

'We'll call soon,' I said. 'We must dash.' And we hurried out before she could begin to ask questions. She'd report this to the police, I knew, but Alison's life might be saved. That mattered to me, a lot.

'Where do we go now?' asked MacIntyre. 'I wanted to be at my safe police station—they obviously knew that.'

'Let's go somewhere quiet, sir, where we can think,' I suggested. 'We've got to get clear of the town first. They'll give it

285

a thorough going-over if they think we're still here.'

'What about him?' he indicated Riley in the rear. I'd momentarily forgotten him in my concern for Alison. I examined him briefly. He was dead; there was no doubt about that. He'd caught a bullet in the head, and his pulse was non-existent.

'He's beyond human aid,' I told Mac-Intyre. 'We'll have to get rid of this car and find another. You've got to be in Newcastle for Monday morning, haven't you? That means you must hide for a full day.'

'There's my wife too,' he said softly. 'They took her, remember.'

'Have you any idea where she'll be?'

'No, I'm sorry. I mustn't let that affect my judgement and of course I must attend the meeting as arranged in spite of her abduction.'

I started the engine and drove from the hospital grounds. I took the minor road up to Bullamoor, for this led to a quiet stretch of countryside on rising ground. It was a good place to reconsider our situation and to observe the roads below. I turned right at the Fox and Hounds Inn at Bullamoor and a mile or so further on, I pulled up in a dark lane where I switched off all our lights.

'I want to search Riley,' I told MacIntyre. 'Somehow he put them onto our trail.'

In the dim glow of the interior light, I hauled him, still bleeding, on to the rear seat and began to rifle his clothing. Apart from the expected personal belongings like money, comb, handkerchief and keys, he did have a small radio set. It was similar to the one I'd seen Megson use in London, but was of a different colour and of a slightly different style. It was alive now, burbling very softly. One had to put it very close to one's ear to listen or to transmit. I felt our conversation in the car would not have been picked up by this set.

'Have you seen these things before?' I lifted it up for MacIntyre to examine.

He nodded. 'Yes, it's similar to the type used by the Security Service. It's a two-way radio, that's all, and can be tuned into one of several frequencies. I think there'll be a bugging device too. They do that, you know, so they can trace the movements of suspect vehicles.'

'On him, you mean?'

'It's very possible. If so, they'll be able to follow us. It takes time, though, because the device gives only an approximate area and has a limited range. Once they find us they can follow easily; let's hope we're out of their range now.'

Already I was searching thoroughly. There were no microphones in his clothing but when I opened his shirt, I found the webbing straps about his torso and the battery operated bug at his waist. It was about the size of a stick of rock—say ten inches long by an inch in diameter. It was this device which relayed a signal to their car and which would be interpreted by their sensitive machinery. Many people think these bugs are small and easily concealed, but this is not so. Not yet, anyway.

'Leave him here,' MacIntyre said. 'We'll have to get away quickly—someone will find his body but bring his radio set. We'll throw that bug into a field somewhere— that'll mislead them!'

We dumped the body behind a hedge and made steps to get away from the scene as quickly as possible. I turned left along a minor road past Sowerby Grange where I cast the homing device into a stream. Our road led via Kirby Sigston to the A.19 trunk road.

'Park up somewhere, Metcalfe,' said

MacIntyre. 'I'd like to listen to their radio. We'll be safe for some time now that we've thrown away that bug.'

It took us a couple of minutes to drive up to Osmotherley where I drove down a track between two sturdy houses in the village and parked behind one of them, nicely out of sight.

We turned up Riley's radio and listened.

TWENTY

When switched to full volume, we could hear voices and soon it was clear that they were organising the hunt for us. There was a male at 'control' and I did not know his identity nor his location. Other voices, male and female, were making use of the medium and it seemed we had joined them during a roll-call.

This radio was typical of those used by many police forces for observation purposes; the master set would be portable and battery operated and it would be possible to use one of many frequencies, and then to be totally independent of the major police radio networks. The master set, wherever it was, was on 'talk-through' because we could hear all the out-going calls and their responses; normally, when listening to police radios, one can hear one half of every conversation, that is the half emitted by Control. The replies of the men in the field are inaudible but this was not so here, fortunately.

We heard Northallerton mentioned several times and after listening carefully, we realised that we had managed to dispose of their Number Seven, Riley. The calls for him were repeated many times and it was highly probable they knew he was in our car or in our hands, but I felt his death would not be known to them.

I was sorely tempted to respond as Number Seven in order to lead them further astray but desisted for the time being upon MacIntyre's advice. Now that we had one of their sets, we could follow their plans and this may give some clue to the whereabouts of Mrs MacIntyre. They in turn would concentrate on finding us, relying heavily on the bugging device we had disposed of.

We remained behind that cottage in Osmotherley for over an hour listening to their frantic search not eight miles away; they'd given Northallerton town a most thorough going-over and had eventually made contact with the bug. One of their cars was in that area, we discovered, and it was making a thorough search to pinpoint its exact position. From its repeated requests for information, we knew it was having difficulty.

I smiled at their efforts, but all this was superfluous information and of no real benefit to us. I hoped to learn the origin of those 'police' cars but received no information which would assist me in that matter. However, after listening to their spasmodic chatter, one important factor did emerge. The master set and their 'control' point must be fairly close to Northallerton; it had to be, to give reception to those pocket radios. Their radius would not be more than ten miles and probably much less, although I mustn't forget that the master set was portable. It may even be in a car itself.

After another half-hour, much of the radio activity ceased; a new voice, speaking to all personnel, said he would have to inform Number One of MacIntyre's escape and disappearance, and he sought the approval of all operatives before taking that action. He asked them to give their answer, yes or no. Clearly it was a democratic organisation!

He began with Number Three; it was clear that Number Two was now doing the talking. Three said 'Yes,' and as he went through the numbers in ascending order, MacIntyre snatched the set from me. 'I'll be Number Seven,' he laughed. 'If they realise he's missing, they should conclude that we are in possession of his radio. That will make them ultra-cautious about their talking, and we might miss a lot. I can imitate his southern accent.'

He practised briefly with the set, pressing the 'speak' button to release the aerial. Number Six had expressed agreement.

'Number Seven?' came the voice, hopefully.

'Number Seven,' said MacIntyre, in a passable imitation of Riley's voice and accent. 'I agree.'

There was a long pause, and then Number Two said, 'What is your location, Number Seven?'

'I am in a field about two miles out of Northallerton,' said MacIntyre, winking at me. 'I was bound by Metcalfe and dumped here. I've just managed to free myself.'

'Where is MacIntyre?'

'He was taken away in the Ford Capri, with the girl and Metcalfe. They talked of heading south, to Thirsk.'

'Received. Can you find your way back to base?'

'Yes,' said MacIntyre.

'Number One will want a full report from you.'

'Received and understood. Number Seven out.'

He looked at me, leaving the set alive in his hands, and asked, 'Was that O.K?'

'I think it would pass for him over the air, sir. I wonder if they use any pass words or coded phrases?'

'I don't know. I didn't detect any during the past hour or so. Perhaps they think their radio network is safe? It is, of course, until someone loses a set! Number Seven's "return" should keep them happy for a short time. Don't forget that the local police will also be hunting them—the Chief Constable will have spoken to Gregory by this time and so this mob can't show themselves too much. That aids us somewhat.'

'Do you wish to lie low, sir, or should we seek your wife?'

'I ought to hide and make sure I get to Newcastle. That's all that's left for me now, Metcalfe. What can they do with my wife, eh? They can't contact me to bargain with me, can they? So what's the use of keeping her now?'

'To blackmail you into not attending that conference?'

'I can't succumb to that, Metcalfe. Even if my wife's life is at stake, I must attend. It is vital to our country and maybe to the whole of the Western way of life.'

'You have a full day left, sir, in which to hide and in which we might find her. Have I your permission to try?'

'Yes, of course I'd be grateful. You know that. But I cannot join the search—I must give priority to my duty.'

'Where can you go for today, sir? I could take you to my own house, but that's not wise.'

'Thank you for the offer. I'll have to keep away from all my friends, relations, acquaintances and regular haunts. It's approaching six o'clock isn't it? I've just over twenty-four hours to keep out of their way. I may need you, Metcalfe, to make sure that I do get there.'

'I'm willing to help,' I said. As we sat there, I told him all about the aircrash, about Alison's role and Thompson. Whilst we chatted, the radio continued to burble in the background, asking more agents for their views. There was a total of twenty-five, but no locations were given. Twenty-five of the bastards in this tiny, rural area, all engaged in a plot to lead this green and pleasant land to disaster. I didn't think for a minute that they were resident operatives; surely, for an exercise of this nature, they would have been imported to the district? Perhaps they operated as a unit, being despatched to differing parts of the country as and when required, stirring up strikes, public disorder and the like?

As we lapsed into silence, I listened to Number Two's voice. Soon his identity registered in my mind. Herriott! He was number Two. I listened intently, for there was some distortion of the signals, but it was him all right. Second-in-command!

So who was Number One?

Herriott, a spy operating within our own Security Service, was soon to report to someone superior to him. He was having to approach his boss on bended knee to report a failure, and none of his operatives could help. If they could, they would have offered over the air and thus saved his face. MacIntyre had beaten them; Herriott had failed and was alone.

He must shortly put in his call to Number One. It was highly probable that few, if any, of the field operatives knew the identity of their Number One. Like our own Security network, they may work in units or cells of two or three, with only one of the cell having personal contact with another cell.

'If we could identify Number One, Metcalfe,' smiled MacIntyre, 'the Government would be eternally grateful to us. He's clearly someone of considerable importance and influence.'

'And,' I said, 'He's not far from us at this minute, is he? If Herriott is going to contact him by radio ...'

'I don't think he will, it's far too risky, my lad. After all, *we* are listening in.'

'But he doesn't *know* that, sir. He thinks this set is in Riley's care, doesn't he? Besides, it doesn't matter who listens in, does it? Even if he speaks to his Number One, we won't know who it is, nor will his own agents.'

'We could find out in time, if they keep transmitting. The Home Office or the Post Office radio people could eventually track down their transmitter, even if it is moved occasionally.'

'All that takes time, sir, so my guess is that they move its location as often as is feasible.'

'I agree, so let's keep listening. That's the only way we might obtain some clues.'

Herriott had ended his transmission and signed off with 'Number Two to stand-by.'

We waited. Ten or fifteen seconds elapsed before he reopened the channel.

'Number Two to Number Seven, are you receiving? Over.'

'That's you!' I nudged MacIntyre.

'Oh God, so it is! Has he tumbled to it?' he put the set close to his mouth and speaking softly, acknowledged receipt of the call.

Herriott repeated his call.

'Number Two to Number Seven, your location please.'

I whispered to him, for him to repeat, 'I'm walking towards the Fox and Hounds Inn, Bullamoor, and eventually Northallerton.'

He copied my words in the cockney accent.

'I'll collect you at the Inn, Number Seven, in say half-an-hour. I'll be in my car.'

'Received,' smiled MacIntyre, 'and thanks.'

'This is our chance!' I said. 'I'll be there to meet him. He'll be going to meet his master, head bowed and full of shame to say that he's failed. I'll bet Riley, Pierce and Mortimer were one cell, taking orders from Herriott. Herriott's on his own because we've got the rest—he's looking for moral support and he wants it from his old pal, Riley. Riley's dead too, but he doesn't know that yet. It'll shatter him completely when he finds out.'

'You could be walking right into a trap. Do you realise that?'

'I do, but we can't ignore this opportunity, can we? If we drive there now and park behind the pub, we can keep our eyes open. If Herriott is alone, we can deal with him. It's still dark enough to conceal ourselves.'

'Deal with him, Mr Metcalfe? What do you mean?'

'Force him to take us to meet his boss.

That's where he's going, to meet Number One in person. He's hoping to take Riley to give his story about how we bulldozed our way out of that road block; he said that over the air, didn't he? He said Number One would want a full report from Riley. I think he's a very frightened man, Mr MacIntyre, and he's very worried.'

'I daren't risk it. I'm free at last. If it is a trap, I must not risk being caught. There's too much at stake.'

'Then let me do it. I'll go alone and you can remain in hiding. I'll need this car to drive there; you can have it afterwards.'

After failing to dissuade me, he said, 'As you wish. I'll drive you there immediately and then I'll disappear. I'm sorry to have to do this; I don't like leaving you to fight my battles or to take risks on my behalf.'

'I understand, sir, but I must do this. I may find your wife, too.'

'Thank you, that would be nice. Let's go now.'

I drove back through the lanes, heading towards Bullamoor and I kept the stolen radio activated. All activity had ceased, for Herriott, having lost his quarry, appeared to have conceded defeat. I was dropped about a mile from the inn and MacIntyre said he would return to Osmotherley and drive on to the moors where he would spend his time, with the radio, before heading for Newcastle. There were plenty of hiding places in those hills and a good pub or two if he chose to take the risk. He was alone, but he was armed. He shook hands and thanked me before driving off.

I walked in the early morning mist and kept well into the side of the road. At the picturesque little pub I found cover from where I could watch all four roads which met at this point. Each was a very minor road, little more than the width of a car and I had only five minutes to wait.

At six-twenty, a Morris 1100 crept towards the cross-roads and came to a halt on the forecourt of the inn, where he switched off all the lights. I could see that the driver was alone, but the darkness prevented me making a positive identification. I waited; I'd make him sweat a little and saw him peering anxiously around. Eventually, he lit a cigarette.

In the flickering flame of his lighter, I recognised the features of Herriott. It was time to go. I hurried on tip-toe to the passenger door, glad of the cover of darkness, and I had my automatic ready.

As I approached, I glanced into the rear compartments; all were empty. He was alone. I made for the passenger door, the front one. My hand gripped the handle and he hadn't noticed me yet. I pressed the catch, hoping to God it wasn't locked.

It wasn't. With a click, the door opened. The courtesy light came on and I revealed myself, showing the Walther to him. He showed no surprise and no emotion, but looked at me with sad eyes.

'I thought this might happen. Where's Riley?'

I settled on the seat beside him, making sure I kept him covered and left the door open to maintain the light. 'He's dead,' I said. 'He was shot through the head, by your own men in that ambush.'

'But I was speaking to him ...'

'No,' I spoke softly. 'You were speaking to myself and Mr MacIntyre. Riley died long before that. Now, Mr Herriott, you are going to take me to your Number One—and I want to find Mrs MacIntyre too.'

'And if I refuse?'

'Then you'll have to die, Mr Herriott. I'll dump your body next to your mate, Riley. He's only a mile or so from here.'

He sat at the wheel, a dejected man, smoking deeply as he stared into the darkness outside.

'It was a foolish thing to do,' he said. 'Me, I mean. My career, my country, my family. I've let them all down.'

'You didn't enter this voluntarily?' I wanted him to talk.

'No. I got into debt. They found out and I began to feed information to them, for cash. It wasn't very useful stuff because I'm fairly low in the hierarchy of the Security Service, but I knew all the ropes and I was very careful. I spent their bloody money. I spent it and got deeper into debt, so I asked for more. They wanted better information in return—they'd got me, Mr Metcalfe. The whole bloody thing snowballed. I'm a traitor, Mr Metcalfe, make no mistake about it. A cowardly bloody traitor who is going to receive the bulling of his life. I'm inefficient too; I'm a failure. I'm a failed traitor! They gave me this job because of my connections within the police and Government Security and I've failed. I'm useless—your lot has been on to us the whole bloody time, right from the start. Thompson, Alison Jenkins, Gregory, you. I told my bosses but they made me go ahead. It could only lead to failure. I told them ...'

'What's in it for you now?' I asked tenderly.

'Misery and utter disgrace. I've failed both sides and no one will want me. I'll be branded as a traitor and I will be handed over to your side, they'll make sure I'm arrested. I'll go to court, there'll be publicity and I'll be gaoled. That's what's in store for me, Mr Metcalfe. I was going to take Riley with me, hoping he'd give me a bit of Dutch courage and that he might explain that I wasn't as useless as all that. I can't even do that, can I? I can't flee—there's nowhere to go. What's left, you might ask? Nothing. There's nothing left.'

'Who is your boss?'

He regarded me closely.

'They're bastards, Mr Metcalfe. They've had me, body and soul, for the past four years. Every move I've made has been monitored, everything I did was watched, every one of my friends was checked. Every letter I wrote and phone call I made was read and checked. I did my best, but my heart wasn't in it. Mr MacIntyre will blow everything, you know. He'll tell the Governments of the E.E.C. just who they are and what they're trying to achieve, how they're trying to destroy Western freedom by gaining power in so many sections of society and industry. And bloody good luck to him.'

'Who is your Number One?' I tried again. 'Tell me—they've got Mrs MacIntyre too.'

He nodded slowly. 'It's going to appear in today's Sunday papers as a blackmail demand. They'll say she's being held hostage so that MacIntyre is forced to pay £50,000 to charity. Instructions will be given of course, through the press. But it's not that at all—they want poor old MacIntyre to go alone to recover his wife and then they'll kill him. It's all worked out. They wanted him alive, to bleed him dry of all his knowledge, but it's too late now. He's got to die.'

'He won't go to collect his wife,' I said. 'I've just left him. He puts his country first, Mr Herriott. He made a great show of telling me that. He won't bite. He's prepared to leave his wife to her fate.'

'I suppose deep down I wanted you to catch me like this. I think, subconsciously, that I didn't want to betray my country and I'm pleased our plot failed.'

'Your Number One?' I still hadn't extracted this vital piece of information. 'Who is he? What's his name?'

He said nothing as he gazed into space, a pale man who was shaking visibly. His hands were on the steering wheel, gripping the rim so tightly that the whites of his knuckles could be seen.

'Mrs MacIntyre? Where is she?' I touched him in the ribs with the muzzle of the Walther.

'You'll find her at Marton Abbey Cottage,' he said. 'Be careful, it's guarded.'

'Come with me.'

I saw his teeth; I saw them flash in the low light as they bit on that thing in his mouth and before I could do anything to save him, he was dying horribly. The strychnine attacked his nervous system and he was paralysed within seconds; death followed almost immediately.

The poor devil! What a torment he must have lived through but there was no time for sentiment. I needed a car—this car. I hoisted his corpse into the rear passenger seat, hoping to God no one saw me, and drove to the point where I had dumped Riley. I left Herriott's body beside that of his pal—when this was all over, I'd ring the police, anonymously, so they would locate the corpses.

Now I had Herriott's car.

The Abbey, now derelict and merely a heap of old stones, had provided the materials for the construction of many local houses. It lay only a couple of miles from here and I drove there like the wind; at the gate was a notice directing callers to the cottage which lay almost a mile along a rough track. I drove carefully showing full headlights because this car was known to them. There was no need for secrecy, but upon arrival my action would have to be swift and sure.

Marton Abbey Cottage was a picturesque place with mullioned windows and a rather squat, solid appearance. It was used chiefly as a summer residence; situated on the banks of the Cod Beck, it was secluded and enjoyed views over some of Yorkshire's finest countryside.

I pulled into the little yard behind the house. Lights were burning inside and none illuminated this yard. I manoeuvred the car into a position for a rapid get-away and as I busied myself the back door opened and there appeared a man.

He was carrying a rifle.

TWENTY ONE

I continued my manoeuvres with the car and finally positioned it so that the headlights shone directly into his face. He covered his eyes with his free hand and at that moment, I drew the Walther from my pocket.

If I allowed the engine to run much longer, he'd grow suspicious so I switched it off and climbed out, but left the headlights blazing. Only when I was fully out did I switch them off, knowing that he'd be momentarily dazzled. It was those few seconds that were so vital.

I was too far away to despatch him with my automatic—these guns are so inaccurate over a distance, and he had a rifle. That *was* accurate, certainly over this range. As the lights went out, the cottage yard was plunged into an area of total blackness. I scurried away from the car. He must have realised it wasn't Herriott; he called, 'Who's there?'

'Number Two,' I replied, hopefully.

I was near a washhouse and saw him emerge from the doorway to seek me. My response hadn't fooled him; his eyes would be rapidly adjusting to the darkness and he had the rifle at the ready. I was now to his left, peeping around the wall.

'Show yourself!' he called, stepping towards the car. 'The driver's door had remained open as I'd run away. He thought I was hiding behind it.

'Here!' I shouted and leapt out, only ten feet from him, with the Walther blazing. Two shots buried themselves in his body, spun him off his feet and kicked him off balance. He hit the ground, stone dead. Within split seconds, I took possession of his rifle, slipped the hot Walther into my pocket and ran into the cottage.

Upstairs I heard running footsteps. A man's voice was calling, 'Ron? Was that you?'

I made no response as I concealed myself in the deep shadows beneath the oak staircase. The caller came clattering down. 'Ron?' he was shouting. 'Where are you?'

I was just inside the door, in a hallway; the hall light was on and I looked for the switch. It was over to my left, on the left of the door as I'd entered. It was too far for me to reach now and I prayed the shadows of the house would hide me.

He came past me and looked outside; I heard his stifled cry as he saw the body lying in the yard. He didn't make the elementary mistake of rushing outside to his friend's aid, but ducked back inside and slammed the door, bolting it securely.

'Eric?' he shouted upstairs. 'We've been raided. Get yourself out of bed.'

He passed very close to where I crouched and presented an ideal target; as he stepped past I rose from my position and swung the rifle around my head, holding the tip of the barrel in my hands. But he heard my movements and ducked. His acute sixth sense had saved the day and he turned to face me. I saw the long-barrelled revolver in his hands.

I kicked viciously at him, hoping to knock away the fearsome weapon but in my panic I misjudged my aim and he pulled the trigger. There was a tremendous retort as a bullet lodged in the oak panelling behind me. How it missed I'll never know—I'd just swayed out of its reach. I ran, putting out the hall light as I did and entered the lounge where I ducked behind a huge settee. It was almost dark in here; no lights burned but in the dawn of this new day I tried to locate him, cocking my rifle as I looked.

But he'd vanished; there was total silence down here while upstairs I heard renewed activity. His mate was coming. I remained absolutely still behind the protection of the furniture as my ears strained to catch and identify any sound. He was doing the same. Upstairs the one called Eric was moving and I heard him call, 'Ron? Peter? What's going on?'

I heard him go to the landing window and draw back the curtains to cry, 'God Almighty!' He retraced his steps to a point just above my head. I could hear him talking to someone and a woman's voice replied, but I couldn't catch their words. He came away from her, his feet sounding loudly on the bare boards above. He began to descend the stairs and switched on the hall light. Its orange glow flooded into this room.

I couldn't see Peter, the man with the long-barrelled revolver, yet he must be here, hiding like me, squatting behind the furnishings. His mate began to descend; Peter, stalking me, wouldn't dare shout a warning because his voice would reveal his whereabouts. He'd let his pal walk to his death, knowing I'd shoot and thus reveal my position. But I had to shoot to reduce the odds. I dropped to the floor and lay flat and out of sight where I adopted the prone position. The rifle was steady in my hands. Through the open door I could see the legs of the newcomer as he came slowly down those stairs. The bannister rails provided some protection, but there were gaps. I took aim.

The action of my breathing caused the tip of the barrel to rise and fall so I ceased to breathe, holding my breath until I squeezed the trigger. My firearm was under control; I waited until I could see the lower portion of his trunk and then his rib cage ...

I knew I'd reveal my position but had no alternative. I couldn't take on two of them. The rifle was automatic, I found, and I had him in my sights. I could pick out the position of his heart and squeezed the trigger. He gave a sharp cry as he pitched headlong down the stairs as, simultaneously, I rolled from my firing position to a new place behind an armchair. No one had fired at me, but the man with the long-barrelled revolver was still in this room. There was not a sound from him.

Those weapons are so clumsy in appearance but so deadly and accurate and I felt completely vulnerable. Although the hall light was burning, it was comparatively dark in here with lots of shadows and he must know my approximate position. I crouched in the shelter of that chair and removed the Walther from my pocket. I made a rapid check and found I had two shots left; I also had the rifle with an unknown quantity of rounds in its magazine but in this confined space I might find the short-range Walther more adaptable. Taking care not to make a sound, I lay the rifle at my side and waited in absolute silence.

The time dragged as I waited; then the fellow I'd shot on the stairs began to groan. He wasn't dead after all and this seemed to be the cue for the woman upstairs to call, 'Hello? What's happening? This is Mrs

MacIntyre. I'm here, quite safe. Hello?'

No one answered. Unless one of us made a move we'd be here all day. I strained my eyes in an effort to pierce the shadows and carefully began to trace the outlines of every piece of furniture. I hoped to spot his bulk; he may be hidden in a dark corner which may create a more intense area of blackness. As I searched, I realised he'd be just as nervous as I, or even more so because I'd eliminated two of his colleagues. Conversely, he'd know the house better than I; it was a big room, two or even three smaller ones knocked together, and it contained excellent furnishings, much of them antique. I could distinguish the solidity of a grand piano, several easy chairs, a coffee table and a cabinet but over here, in my corner, it was completely dark. Could he see into this darkness?

Neither of us dared make a move to bring up the lights and I had to distract him. I needed something to throw. I groped in the chair and discovered a small round cushion. It was yellow in colour and nestled in the back and I gingerly eased it out, drawing it towards me and hoping to cast it from me to attract his fire. I weighed it in the palm of my hand, then raised it to fling it the length of the room.

He'd known where I lay and had been waiting for some movement; there was an almighty crack and two bullets thudded into the wall behind me, sending a cascade of plaster to the floor and one of them carried that cushion from my hand! He'd mistaken it for my head ... God! He was accurate all right!

Three shots gone. He was not far away; he was somewhere in those shadows just inside the door and then I heard movements from Mrs MacIntyre. Her bare feet were padding the floor above and I saw her shadow at the head of the stairs. I wanted to shout a warning but delayed too long because she began her descent. She came into view, a woman in late middle-age, fully dressed except for her shoes.

She saw the shot man at the foot of the stairs and screamed; my concealed gunman shouted to me, 'Come out or I'll drop the woman! If you don't show yourself, she dies. Stay right where you are, Mrs MacIntyre, or you'll die too.'

I thought I recognised that voice but couldn't put a name to it. He'd have to move a fraction to get a clear aim at her and I could see his outline, a dark anonymous figure and the low light glinted from the barrel of that peculiar pistol. That he was a marksman was not in doubt and she was directly in his line of fire. He couldn't miss. I clutched the Walther in my right hand as I retrieved the rifle. Did he know I had two firearms?

'Come out!' he shouted. 'You've got five seconds!'

I watched carefully; if he wanted to kill me he'd have to change his aim very rapidly. There was a chance I could still beat him.

'I'm coming,' I called. He'd have to move his gun-arm through an arc of ninety degrees to hit me. My eyes never left his pistol.

'Stand up and throw down your gun, then walk into the middle of the floor.'

I obeyed; the Walther was in the palm of my right hand and I prayed the darkness would conceal its presence. He'd see the rifle in my left.

'Throw down the rifle—in the middle of the floor.'

I stooped and put it on the carpet, sliding it into the centre of the room. The

Walther slid into a firing position. From his pistol, he had fired three shots. If it was a six-round revolver, which was highly probable, he may have three left. With his standard of accuracy, every one would find its mark. He could destroy both of us and still have one shot in reserve.

'Walk into the middle of the floor,' his weapon was still pointing at Mrs MacIntyre. I moved closer to him; I was still in the shadows and moving gingerly. I had to be close if I was to be sure of hitting him. I was ten feet away.

'It's all over,' I said to him. 'Herriott is dead, Riley is dead and your organisation has been blown completely open.'

'But I will get away,' and in a flash he turned towards me. I was ready and leapt hard to my right, throwing myself to the floor as his clumsy firearm spewed another two rounds. Both dug into the floor where I'd been standing. He'd not followed my movement and I realised he couldn't hit a moving target. That he was a marksman was beyond all doubt but with that sort of pistol, he was a target man! I should have recognised the type of gun, for it was a target pistol, the sort you use on indoor ranges in club competitions.

'Get away!' I shouted at the terrified woman. 'Go back upstairs!'

As I shouted, I released one of my precious shots. It missed and brought a chunk of plaster from the wall behind him. That left one shot each.

I had to keep moving and I had to get close.

I was within his view as he moved about the house, my sensitive finger alert to the pressure of the Walther's trigger. He circled too, realising that I'd recognised his weakness and he wanted to corner me. I began to close in like a weasel hypnotising a trapped rabbit. My only hope was speed and movement; I began to push the chairs about. They moved freely on smooth castors and I shoved them towards him to frustrate his aim. I kept moving, always having a chair between myself and him, hoping it would at least reduce the velocity if one of his pile-drivers came my way.

Then there was a car outside!

We heard it at the same time; it distracted his attention too, for just a fraction of a second and in that time, I pressed the trigger. I felt the Walther jump in my hand as he collapsed with a bullet in the shoulder of his gun arm. It was a lucky shot.

'Stay right there, or the next is in your head,' I threatened with my empty gun.

'Don't kill me,' he pleaded as I collected the deadly pistol from the floor where he'd dropped it. More cars arrived and I picked up the rifle.

'It's safe now, Mrs MacIntyre,' I shouted upstairs. 'You can come down.'

The car had contained Mr Gregory and his fellow agents. Another car contained Special Branch detectives and Mrs MacIntyre was taken away. It took all morning to clear up the place, and the fellow who'd been shot on the stairs died later. Peter survived, but with a smashed shoulder; he was swiftly taken away by the Security Service and I never saw him again.

When I found time, I rang the Friarage Hospital on the cottage telephone and learned that Alison was not seriously hurt. She'd lost a lot of blood from a deep flesh wound but should recover perfectly. I left a message to say I'd call to see her as soon as I could.

As I read the Sunday papers in the Fox and Hounds Inn at Bullamoor that lunch-time, I saw that a Socialist member of Parliament, who was a member of the Shadow Cabinet, had unexpectedly resigned and the reason was given as 'ill-health'. I asked Gregory if that man was the subject of the counter-plot they'd been working upon. He merely smiled. 'We do our best to weed the subversives from all parties', he said with a gleam in his eye. 'They infiltrate at all levels to gain power, albeit in an undercover way. There are some in the Government, you know, and many in the Opposition. There is one less now. As a matter of interest,' he continued, 'that cottage was rented by that particular M.P. It was he who you fought—he's a crack shot with a pistol. But of course, none of this will reach the papers.'

I knew I'd heard that voice before? I've heard it so many times on television but had never obtained a good view of his face in that cottage. I learned afterwards that he'd been wearing a wig anyway!

The Sundays gave a splash to the supposed kidnapping of Mrs MacIntyre and the ransom demanded, but we could ignore that now. As I downed my final pint, I realised I had a lot to tell Mrs

Thompson. Riley had killed her husband because he'd learned too much about this job, but also to retrieve the money which had been borrowed for the occasion. She would receive an adequate pension from the Government; he had worked well because he'd deliberately allowed Alison's car to be traceable. That, above all, had sealed the fate of the plotters.

I did wonder what would have happened if I'd kept the £25,000, or if they'd chosen someone other than Thompson? But I didn't want to think any more about it. The beer was good, and as I drank it I realised I'd never given a thought to that murderous grey saloon that had dominated my life until last Sunday.

Tomorrow I'd renew the hunt, and tonight there would be a raid on a small sub-post office in Swaledale. I couldn't be bothered to call it off.

Besides, in fifteen minutes it was visiting time at the Friarage Hospital.